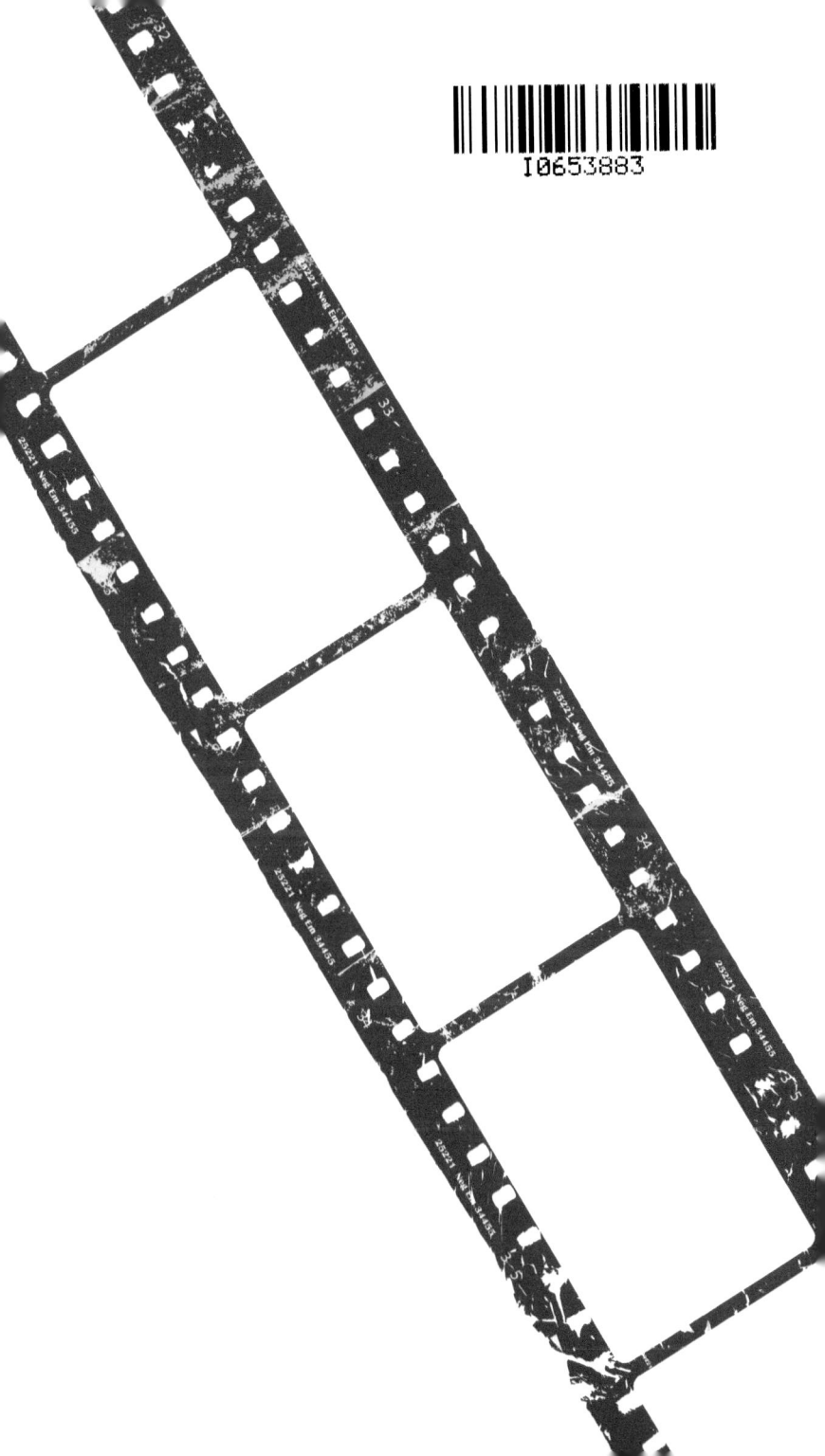

STELLIFY

Neilan

Cover design by Aaron Kent

Edited & Typeset by Aaron Kent

Broken Sleep Books (2022)

Broken Sleep Books Ltd
Rhydwen,
Talgarreg,
SA44 4HB
Wales

Contents

i.

\a process of becoming\   11
\teenage actress\   19
\rom-coms\   23
\star creature\   25
\isabelle\   33

ii.

\the danish woman\   39
\the moon also rises\   55
\stuntman\   63
\the corpses\   65
\the sound of glass almost breaking\   73
\auditions\   75
\the psychological thriller\   77
\sad hitmen\   83
\jean\   85

iii.

\re-education\   89
\the hall of the mountain queen\   95
\kittisak\   107
\delicacy\   117

iv.

\seventeen hours in copenhägen\   121
\kim basinger\   127
\star creature 2: genesis\   135
\sandrine\   141
\girth\   143
\for sale\   149
\all the chases\   157

v.

\ the hills \   161
\ making dinner for andriy tarkovsky \   163
\ peach \   191
\ dana carvey \   201
\ henning \   207
\ lindsay \   217

vi.

\ that's that \   221
\ all the people you've ever loved,   223
or a process of unbecoming \   223
\ jimmie's show \   227
\ jazz bar \   243

vii.

\ santeria \   251
\ hong kong action remake \   255
\ ruan lingyu \   265
\ star creature 3: return of star creature \   269
\ the place in silverlake \   273
\ press screening \   277
\ partial resolution \   281

Acknowledgements   283

Stellify

Chris Neilan

My God---

It's full of stars

i.

\ *a process of becoming* \

IN THE movie I have elephantitis. Elephantitis is the enlargement or hardening of limbs caused by the obstruction of lymphatic vessels. The writer has not researched elephantitis.

You've become huge, he tells me, but you are locked inside your hugeness. The writer is Danish and Syrian. His English is unlike the others'--flavoured with unexpected flourishes and reformulated consonants. The others speak English with accents as flat and clear as the water by the Strait of Øresund. They drink two beers in the evenings, no more: there is important work to be done. They hover around the writer and director, in their sweaters and gillets, carefully looping extension cable. The director looks like a Mads Mikkelsen boychild. All the men in Copenhägen look like some alternative version of Mads Mikklelsen. On the Mikkelsen scale, the director is a 7.

The writer tells me that my hugeness has crept up on me, and then, all of a sudden, taken over my body, devouring me, billowing out around the old lines of me like yeast, bone and muscle and sinew eating me up, my body a loaf over-levened in an oven left on. It would have started slowly, he tells me, something noticed from an early age, hard patches that should have been soft, tough pillows of tissue in crevices

11

and joints, but it would have been little more than an irritant, an embarassment, until I started to spill over my own lines, to accelerate, the very skull growing on one side like a tree straining for the light, the minerals starfishing, redoubling, double-clicking, copy-and-pasting, until I am what I see before me. I look in the mirror. The make-up job is good — the European Film Board has provided generous funding. Layers upon layers of mottled silicon. Underneath the layers, smoothed with foundation at the join, are my eyes, and the flats of skin below my eyes; a good forty percent of my nose, supporting the rotten bulb that they've attached; a slant of one side my mouth, adjoining the enlarged silicon lips; my own bony, creviced, angled chin. Lopsided ordinarily, it slopes pereceptibly to the right. It is now in accord with the extended balcony of my cranium.

You were a sad an lonely man before all this, the Writer tells me, an *now...* he shrugs his shoulders. He has a patchy beard—not uncharmingly patchy—and the eyes of a distrustful red setter. He is not without handsomeness. Now, of course, he says, now... is much, much more.

I have researched elephantitis, however, so I know that the script is hokum. Elephantitis, for example, almost always affects the limbs or genitals, not the skull or face. Elephantitis is unlikely, also, to be accompanied by super strength. This is a conversation I had fleetingly with Henning, the director. The conversation can be summarised as follows:

* it's a movie

* no-one knows what elephantitis is and they don't care

* if it seems like it makes sense, it makes sense

I didn't want to argue too hard, since the European Film Board is providing a paycheque of not inconsiderable heft, but also because, though it pained my ordinarily-sized heart to admit it, he had a point. If it seems to make sense, it makes sense. He could not have summed up this global epoch better, this Mads 7 boychild, if he tried. This is something, apparently, that both he and the Danish-Syrian writer were able to accept far more readily than me.

A bony lump grew on the forehead of Joseph Merrick. His spine slipped and curved to the side so much it resembled a petrified serpent. His right femur was broad as a mallet, the knee six inches lower than the left, and if you could see the bone's surface, as the surgeons later would, you would have seen it the colour of half-rotted teeth. His head did not have the look of anything that had grown or expanded, any more than a granite cliff does. It looked, rather, like some great stony edifice that had been cursed with life.

After he was rejected by his father and his stepmother—and there, if you'll agree, is the most perfect summation of the need we all have for a mother's love—he went to live with his uncle, worked in a workhouse. He had one enormous, misshapen arm, two enormous misshapen feet, and that head—the head of some creature of the moon. He had hair. He had eyes and teeth. Imagine the work; imagine the colleagues: other young men, poor and unfortunate and delinquent young men. Joseph eventually sought out a showman. He asked to be put in his freak show. And yes, said the showman, yes Joseph. I have a place for you in my show, poor Joseph of the moon. Did he touch Joseph, the showman? Did he smooth the spartan carpet of his hair? Did he embrace poor Joseph? Did he visit with his uncle? I have a place for your boy, did he tell him? Did his tongue trip on the word boy?

In the fifth scene of the movie I am battling with my own grotesquery. New to the city, my disease has enveloped me, and I feel a crushing desire for the love, or perhaps just the affection, of a woman. So I go to visit a woman of the night. But, perhaps understandably, she rejects me.

You must approach this scene with, uh... ah, you're not some, you're not some like *horny guy*, right? That's not what's going on here, right? This is something deeper. The director—Henning—is frowning his rumply youthful brow at his dog-eared print-out of the script, as if struggling to conjugate a foreign verb. Two other Mikkelsens from the camera department (a 6, a tubby, moustachioed 4) are listening seriously at his shoulder. He has told me previously, Henning, what he wants from me in this scene. De*sire*, he said, emphatically, but it's *sad* desire. It's... you know... and he made a squeezing gesture with both hands. Strangled? Yeah, he shrugged, settling for my interpretation. Strangled desire. The writer had been there, in the periphery. Dressed for winter in a worn cardigan, he was always on the fringe, as these young Mikkelsens took over his story and decided how, with their language of cameras, it should best be told.

He would sit in the lowest chair available, holding a paper cup of tea in both hands, taking in, with his ordinary human face, its steam, and his face would relax, as if, through that steam, his own pending transformation had been stifled. He made no contribution to the discussion of strangled desire, but he explained later the thinking that had given birth to this endeavour: I told to the funding commission that I wanted to write a movie about what it would be like if the elephant man was an immigrant to Copenhägen, he told me. He shrugged his shoulders. And they liked it, so... His sentences often petered out, the way sentences of shy people often do.

I tell the director I understand the character's strangled desire. In the script, the woman of the night is disturbed, cold, but the actress, a blonde local TV actress with an acorn-shaped head and the quality of a new wife, whose schedule precluded rehearsals and who, therefore, I am meeting for the first time, has suggested a change. I cahn't do it like this, she says, with wet eyes. I just— I think she should be kind to him. The director encourages her to try it her way for a couple of takes. She is odd, this woman: as if she has had some recent unravelling in her personal life that she is unable to stop from spilling into this role. You can see her, trying to hold something back, failing. She holds her hand, now and again, up to her mouth, and the hand seems to be shaking. As we perform the scene, she looks into my eyes. In the uppers of my vision I can see the ceiling of my extended brow, can feel the weight on my cheeks, my temples, skewed on the right of my head so that my neck is slanted to that side. I see her seeing this creature, this character, me, and finding it to be real. She is terribly tender. She touches me on the part of the arm that is me, and I feel the clammy warmth of her fingertips. I am crying. I cannot remember what I am supposed to say.

What happened? Henning asks, and I am unable to find an answer. I find I am unable, in fact, to speak.

The make-up artists tell Henning and the producer and the assistant producers that it is quite punishing to be under so much prosthetic, that it is not uncommon for such a thing to take unusual tolls on a performer. I am not sure if they are being honest or just being nice, but I appreciate it nonetheless. Henning and his team are concerned. They say they are concerned about me, although it is quite clear they are mainly concerned about the production. This is simple pragmatism.

The scene, it seemed, had disappeared completely from my head, taking with it all the performance skills that had accrued in the past two decades, all the layers of thickened skin, all the techniques that prevent self-consciousness, and left behind it some scared and naked boy. The actress grew shakier, and comforted me, as I flushed and panicked, as if I was embodying some issue from her own recent experience, as if she were comforting her own treasured husband in crisis. The writer, I saw, had appeared on the fringe of the set, in his cardigan, and from the shadows beyond the set lights was taking it all in. Come on man, he needs a few minutes, Jesus, the actress had said. But it wasn't clear what I needed.

As I sit in the make-up chair, staring at a reflection which no longer seems neither real nor unreal but in some limbo space of infinite existence between the two, the Writer approaches and sits with me. What happen? he asks.

I don't know. It just got away from me.

He nods, as if this makes a kind of sense to him, His eyelashes are long, and his lower lids fringed by faintly darkened lines, that seem to suggest a distant period of sleeplessness. He looks in the mirror, looks away, rubs at the soft, pock-marked skin of his cheeks. I sink you are good actor, he says, making eye contact via the mirror, and I can see beyond him the make-up artists returning. I sink you unnerstan, he says. After he has shuffled out, with a few polite words for the motherly make-up artist, I find that I have located my character's intention.

\ *teenage actress* \

SHE HAS graduated from her initial freckle period to join the ranks of the superstars. Shriek, squeal, pout, strip off, it's a free for all from here. And who's gonna reap those big fat juicy rewards, baby girl? her father says, out of earshot of her mother and her mother's boyfriend. Us, that's who, and he poke-taps the flesh below her collarbone with one of his big sun-crinkled fingers. S'gonna be dreams comin' true time.

So whaddyou wanna be? her manager asks her.

Like… like, you mean like…

Like what *type*, she says. Sexy? Goodie-goodie? Geek chic queen? I can see you stepping into geek chic. I am *not* sure about this sweater, where did you get this? and she tugs the elastic-wool hem with a manicured finger. I like you in scoop necks. And more mascara. Remember the Just 7 shoot? The response to that is what we should aim for. Lotta influencer love for that look. You look flat, your core routine working out? Did Jay hit on you yet? He hits on everyone, he hit on me first session, I said if he did it again I'd cut his dick off. He hits on you, kick him in the scrotum. Unless you wanna fuck him in which case go nuts. Her fifteenth birthday comes and goes, her sixteenth. She puts keepsakes from the shoot in

Sevilla around her room, in the house her mom bought with her money (she has learned not to refer to it as her money). Who's *that*? Janelle asks, pointing at the pictures of Juanito, but that's a secret, that one's just for her and the birds.

If she squints real hard with her eyes closed, she can see pools of light in the darkness—glowing neon red-yellow pools of love. It's cool to have a craft, she tells Dani, like I have this framework I can go to. Mm-hm, for sure, Dani says. Have I told you about the pool of love?

No,

Dani says.

Weeell, it's this pool that emerges from the inside.

When you've known true love.

Like, you can swim around in it. I like to backstroke.

Uh huh,

she says.

I like to dunk my head under in the moonlight and open my Goddamned mouth.

She gets the part, tells herself she'll just avoid the producer, not be in a room alone with him. She puts on weight because the Kraft services table becomes her safe place. Is that a *muffin top*? *Fuck* off Kayla. She entreats herself to try harder. She writes a poem:

> Where beyond the glimmer
> goes my heart?
>
> Where beyond the hearth
> that heats my castle
> goes my love?

Wherefore drifts my love?

She entreats herself to try harder. She commits to learning Spanish. *¿Donde más allá del brillo entra mi corazón?* She looks out for scripts that might shoot in Andalucia. There is a pool, in Andalucia, that she visits, in her dreams, that she knows like the back of her eyelids. It's fringed with bulrushes, jacaranda, scree, and it is always glowing night, and the water is warm at the surface, cool to cold the lower you go, and dark, black, impenetrable—who knows how deep, she can feel it on the bare skin of her legs, her back, and he is splashing in the distant adjoined lagoon, singing

Mi amor va más allá

The nomination is a surprise but won't hurt her prospects one fucking bit. You seem to have a real quality to you, the septuagenarian director tells her, and his spotless sidekicks nod nod nod. That's why we're interested in you. She adjusts her sitting position. Her mother's boyfriend is thumbs-upping through the window. The director assesses her lower body. Yes, he murmurs, yes, and the nodders nod. If you are sexy, you are the world's property, he tells her later, everyone has a right to you. You are Salmacis, you are Daphne... have you read the classics? No? Beauty, you see, beauty... it's so profound. We all must come to look. She learns to accept the things she cannot change, the hands she cannot see coming. She has, after all, her pool.

THE NEUROTIC

sexual predator pursues understanding. He follows his love through the strands of time, he plays with lobsters, he considers the nature of comedy. He is probably a child molester.

The daughter of the executive is played by a great beauty who has not yet become a great beauty. She falls in love with her dad's young boss—a kind of love, perhaps. The father doesn't know what to make of it.

The cameraman with the cast on his wrist is no ad exec, but his heart is made of the right stuff. He'll find her, in the church, when she's sorry—there'll be a scene. Things might work out, they just might. Kevin Bacon's hair is long.

A spectrum of couples have Christmassy dalliances, soft yellow lighting in London houses no earthling could now afford. The southern belle discovers love, discovers herself, studies law, cracks the code. The Hispanic maid develops a sense of self, and boy her man looks nice in a nice pressed shirt.

The couple have met in a previous film—their love is established. But now she runs an independent bookshop, and he's a corporate type. A recent technological development provides the framework. She doesn't know the man she chats to online is really her doe-eyed corporate nemesis, but we do, and we can see where it's going. In the previous film, there was a dead wife. The man's love for her was so beautiful. The actor summoned it, this dead wife love, this spectre of love, on the phone, in front of the kid playing his son, to some woman playing a radio host, and she listened, the actress, playing his distant love interest, listened over a prop radio. She listened as this spectre of love was summoned, and barely had to act. A building-top meet-up on the Empire State was all it took... but now there are these emails, and parks, and bookshop politics, and they're pretending they don't know each other, that they're these other people. But they know, we know, everyone remembers. When they discover what's really going on, and realise what they knew all along, it's this love they're rediscovering, this love between the distant woman and the Seattle widower with the sad son and the dead imaginary wife.

\star creature

THE CRITIC is under-appreciated.
His knowledge has been honed, he knows what he's talking about—fifty shitting quid a shitting article? Wouldn't've been like that in the nineties, people still paid to read stuff then. To be honest, if he can get fifty quid he's lucky. Mostly these days they simply don't pay.

He takes her back to his place, remembering too late that he hasn't cleaned. Rumpled sweaters and chinos on the floor, on the bed, a towel hanging over the back of his computer chair.

It's not usually like this, he says. She takes off her coat.

How would you like to be eaten?

He blinks.

Would you like to be devoured or savoured?

Well, I--

Put that down, you've had enough. Come here. She navigates a backwards path to the bed. This is the universe, do you understand? She smooths the rumpled sheet.

The bed?

It's the universe. There, jump in. She encourages him to dive, corrects his form. I'm going to eat you, she tells him, the lights from the top deck of a passing bus glinting in her eyes. Her eyes are troublingly deep, more than eyes normally are. I'm going to eat every bit of you now, just like you've been dreaming of. You have been dreaming of me, haven't you? Dreaming of me, and your matter, in a feeding frenzy? No frenzy is wrong... I'm going to devour you slowly. Yes lie down, good. She looks not exactly like the person he met at the press screening, but he did have more than a couple of the free glasses of plonk. She asks him, as she massages her jaw, to list his most underrated East Asian films of the past three decades. Well, Hou Hsiao-Hsien... I'm a big flannel of... I'm a flaneuse of... and, Lee Chang Dong is—amongst the roomiest... The ceiling has become a pond. Are those fish?

Yes, she says, without moving her mouth.

Why are there fish in my ceiling? She asks him for his thoughts on Wajda. Hmmmcomplicado. Ha, ha. Mplicated. Cumplicuted. I'm a cinema. Muh. Muh lups. They're not really. Ha. Hm.

The fish are massing, and turning their fish eyes at him. A cloud of infinite fish shifting and turning above him.

He makes them bacon sandwiches, but he's out of ketchup, so uses barbecue sauce. So, you're in Dulwich, right? The one-three-six heads that way, I can walk you. Yes please, in a bit, she says, digging in. She looks slightly different again—a third version. He asks her to tell him about herself. Well, let's see. You already heard about King's, and India, etcetera. Oh—well, I mean—this seems too obvious to say, but, I mean, I'm a star creature. Yes, she tells him, I was formed in the depths of a white giant. I am a star, in a way. Or will be. It's hard to quantify. He watches her peel open the sandwich and squeeze in another stripe of barbecue. So, ghm... so of course I'm well aware of you. I know all there is inside of you. I think you were making us tea?

He attends the press screening of a Turkish docudrama. In the film, a boy of seventeen sells flowers, or tries to, to motorists on the Bosphorus bridge—a cacophonous artery linking Europe and Asia. He taps windows, holds out handfuls of plastic wrapped roses, lifted from a plastic bucket tucked under his arm, and the cars flow by like strange mechanical insects, and he this little figure by the bridge's edge. A lonely police officer tries to find a wife over the internet, and a young married couple search for a house they can afford. Turkish nationalists use a national holiday to march, chant, fly their flags. The flower seller is on the bridge at night, trying to negotiate money from the crawling stream of machines.

He takes her to a Jazz Bar off Wardour Street. It is called: Jazz Bar. There are Christmas lights in the window. A girl in a see-through mack is twirling and twirling and twirling. But I *al*ways get the shit no-one else will review, that's the point. She rolls her eyes, looks around the room, eyes the slender body of the lunatic girl in the see-through coat. He is worried she's going off him, so stops complaining, starts telling his anecdote about the time he saw Mark Kermode at a urinal. Stop trying to impress me, she says, it's boring. Her lips have an anaconda-ish quality. They meet the others in some Tudor pub near Victoria. He watches her conducting

27

the conversation, wrapping them around her little finger. He tries to get some sense out of them whilst she's gone to the toilet, but they're entranced, speak only gobbledigook. I wasn't in the toilets, she says later, and I saw what you were doing. Do you really think I need the toilet? Lie down. No— open your eyes. Look into my mouth. Tell me what you see. No, I don't want to know what you think, I want to know what you can see.

I can see... star matter.

And?

Teeth?

And? Look closer.

He doesn't see her for a while—at least he doesn't think he does. If things are what they seem, she doesn't seem to be around. And it's Christmas, more or less—snow slushing in the streets around Embankment, Charing Cross, bustles on the tube, great crowds of murmuring commuters, slow creeping through the ticket barriers and funnelled through a single exit, grandpa faces on men his father's age, and he feels ancient himself, can feel a hole forming in the sole of his shoe, a cavity forming in a molar. He receives an email from the assistant editor: screening and press conference for the new Soderbergh. Soderbergh will be there, and Waltz, Law, Cotillard. We can pay you a hundred, it says. A thousand word review in the print edition, and a conference piece online. A one-on-one with the director. A real interview.

He shows up at the Clarence after the screening, led out

of the car and guided in by a doorman in a powder blue uniform. The film had been confusing: a byzantine narrative that skipped and double-backed such that he wondered if he'd drifted off, or if the reels had been shown in the wrong order. It had started with a man working for a pharmaceutical conglomerate discovering something potentially scandalous about the side effects of a new product they were developing, but then it had become about a different man in therapy, and his sister, who was having a breakdown. He'd kept expecting the separate strands to merge and conjoin, or at least to become somehow linked, but they never did. Instead a terrorist attack disrupted both of the strands, and there was a sequence following two of the conglomerate's executive officers on a fact-finding trip to Guangzhou. He sees her in the pristine foyer standing next to a decorative fir. What are you doing here?

You're going to fuck this up.

He asks her what she's talking about.

You didn't understand the movie and you're going to fuck this up. She tells him to keep his big mouth shut until she tells him otherwise, and not to make a fool of himself. He is led into the ballroom, where the press are gathered, drinking teas and coffee from white china cups, snacking on good biscuits and cake fingers, and in the adjoined room a stage is set up with chairs and microphones and a background displaying the film's poster and the name of the distribution company.

He hovers anxiously as the other smart and rumpled and serious and collegiate members of the entertainment press masticate and mingle. They seem to belong so much more than him. And she is somewhere—he catches glimpses, flashing her star matter. The sparkling wine shimmers in the London light. When the conference begins, he has no conception of what will happen, but a kind of raw childlike fear has swollen up inside of him, and the sparkling wine has caused a touch of acid reflux. He is seated in the back, behind the first few rows, where Philip French and Jason Solomons and thirty or forty of the most legitimate film critics and reviewers in the country are seated, chatting, turning in their chairs, some still holding onto their teas and coffees, which he didn't know you were allowed to do. A host he recognises from a defunct arts program is in the anteroom, laughing with a production assistant. You're going to do as I say, she whispers into his ear, and he feels his ear flushing, feels the heat spreading to his cheek. He tongues the forming cavity. She is still whispering when three applauding production assistants form an honour guard in the doorway, and the applause ripples through Philip French and the broadsheet critics to the online critics and the bloggers and to him. Soderbergh has not shaved, but his jeans are smooth, his cardigan charming, and he has the impish elven quality of a librarian with a past.

As Soderbergh is interviewed by the recognisable man, the critic experiences something not unlike a flashback, not unlike an out-of-body experience. In fact it is neither—he has sidestepped into a trajectory of his past. He is himself, as an eleven year old boy, and he is running through the mud and the bare trees of the wooded path behind the school playing fields known at the Bog Trot, in his shorts (black, nylon-polyester, the elastic going) with the cuffs of his long-sleeve PE jersey (also the school's rugby and football shirt) pulled over his hands from the cold. Mud is splashed up his legs all the way to his thighs. Other boys are running—similarly kitted figures panting and fallumphing through the bracken. After the run the boys shower in their shorts, scraping the mud from their cold-blotched knees, streams of brown water pooling in the showers' guttering. He has heard rumours that two of the boys were able to spy on the girls' showers, peering through the windows. He is glugging on a Pepsi bottle bong in the hedged part of Lindfield common with the hard kids a year or three later—great gulps of sulphur and ash that go straight to his head. He is seven, and his dad is leaving him. Only, his dad never left him. It is some other dad, leaving some other version of him.

Stand up now, useless man.

He does stand.

Do you know what to say?

He does know what to say.

Soderbergh and the recognisable man and Waltz and Law and Cotillard are looking at him, because this is not the type of event where people stand up in the middle of someone else's question. The recognisable man says something, and Waltz makes a quip at his expense, and there is some laughter, but that's just because they don't know what he's going to say yet.

When he arrives back at his flat, in the shit bit of Wimbledon, the world is a different place. Rippled purple clouds like the inside of an oyster shell have turned the sky into a ceiling. He allows her to do her devouring thing. Now, she says, and for a moment she is silhouetted in front of his blinded window like an illustration from an epic poem or something from a dream, this time I'm going to eat a good big chunk of your soul. Would you like to object? No I thought not. She advises him to count backwards through Sight & Sound's top 100 films of all time to keep him calm, and he does, but only to please her—he doesn't need to. He is perfectly calm. He has been waiting to be eaten up for decades, it turns out.

\ *isabelle* \

'Despite being built up by Melville and a few reviewers as an alternative Brigitte Bardot, she faded from history.'

— Ginette Vincendeau, An American in Paris

HE SEES HER ^{in the} Place

de la Madeleine whilst driving past with his secretary. She is twenty yards away, and fifteen years old, and he likes her at once. He has been auditioning girls for the part all day. Stuck in traffic flow, he sends his secretary out to approach her. Her heels clip-clop the cobbles as she trots, and Isabelle responds to the call, to the hand on the crook of her arm. He sees, in the rearview, below the brim of his *Americain* hat, over the rim of his Ray Bans, as the traffic sweeps him along, that his secretary points out the car, and the girl, getting distant now, fifteen years old, blonde, curvaceous in her sweater and A-line, her hair pinned back, looks, and maybe she sees the shape of his *Americain* hat through the rear window, as he is swept away.

The part is a good one — a coquettish minx lost on the streets of Pigalle. She appears barely two minutes into the feature, catching the eye of the hero, Bob, as she rides off through the glistening Montmarte pre-dawn on an American sailor's scooter, picked up and whisked off for whatever teenage girls in tight sweaters and A-lines are whisked off for by muscular war veterans, and Bob, fifty, laconic, adored by all, watches

33

her with a hint of longing. She comes back the next night, big-eyed and blonde, and wrangles her way into Bob's home. She wants to sleep with him—she makes that clear. Bob, the gentleman, takes care of her instead—puts her to bed, alone. He keeps his desire to have her, her lovely teenage body, on the inside of his fifty-year-old head.

Your character represents the kind of girl who has been around all my life, the director tells her. Very young, very high heels, making no distinction between good and evil. Isabelle nods, nods, listens as he talks, blowing cigar smoke, his hat off and egg-shaped head exposed, his secretary fussing with production assistants beyond. No distinction between good and evil, he says again, and *instantly*—he clicks his fingers in her face—burning their wings under the impression that they are really living. Yes? He is not smiling, and he is waiting for her agreement, which she gives, with a nod, with his large warm hand on her forearm. He seems to enjoy her agreement: he relaxes into his cigar. Beautiful girls, he says, eyeing the distance, dark circles bearing his eyes, his eyes which he so often covers, beautiful girls... who are soon *trapped* and *ground down*—he fixes his eyes on her—by the city of men. Because of course, a city belongs to its men, no?

She has everything it takes to be a big star: beauty, intellect, the right age. He frames her breasts in the bedsheets the way a *patissiere* would frame a *Viennoiserie*. She is, at the time of shooting, sixteen-years-old.

In the feature, she wants Bob, and Bob wants her, but Bob, the much-loved gentleman thief, resists. Instead, he shepherds her into a dalliance with his young protege and son figure, Paulo. They use his studio apartment, with the slanted windows letting in the miasmic Pigalle light, for their rendezvouses. Bob returns one dawn, finds them in the bed, naked under the sheets, asleep, and watches over them with a sort of melancholia—he has got what he planned, shipped them together, the only way it can be, what with him being an honorable man. But he wants the girl. That much is clear. She is a beautiful young girl. And he is still a man. These are the ways of things. And he is a good man.

The director signs her to a long-term contract, but forgets about her. He is a busy man.

ii.

EVERYTHING that matters happens at

3:11am, he says, slurring, into the mic, spicker-echo and feedback bouncing around the glowing box-room, and a neo-ballad about a heartless lover upshifts. Ten minutes later he's vomiting rice-gruel onto the glitter-grained table, but that's the future, and none of us can see that far no matter how we look. Kim Dae Woo is slumped in a corner with the woman he said was his wife but is not his wife, the one he said was his wife's friend but who is not his wife's friend next to them in an arm-folded grump. Dainty little bracelets around her slender wrists.

The previous day I'd been in Jagalchi fish market browsing razor clams when the panic attack had hit. A fist of your own organs closing under your ribcage. I sent a box of blue crabs tumbling, banded claws and lethargic legs skittering on the slopped floor, and all the faces turned (nosed and frowned and eye-bag skewed) my way. I had no guide on hand to explain.

Thing was, I'd been learning my lines:

DANISH WOMAN: Come in— Oh!
THE STRANGER: Please, don't be—
DANISH WOMAN: Wha— what's that over your... over your head?

THE STRANGER: Don't be fraid. I take off in moment.

DANISH WOMAN: Is it... it's— some kind of bag? The hell's your problem? Take it off.

THE STRANGER: Just don't be fraid. I good man.

DANISH WOMAN: Take it off, right now, or I'm calling my boss.

THE STRANGER: I take off, I take off. Just, don't be fraid. Don't be fraid.

I'd been in Busan for twelve hours, cooped up in a neon-signed motel, a street back from Haeundae beach, that I hadn't realised was a love motel, and was yet to see Johan. The adjacent road: a strip of glass-fronted 'massage' places hidden from view by a wall of conveniently placed roadside shrubs. The room: lotus flowers swirling on the walls, complimentary lubricant. It held the echoes of a thousand trysts. I sent my messages: I'm here. Where are u? Let me come and see u. Talk to me please. A worried beagle GIF (an attempt to inject normality). His responses: slow, sporadic, monosyllabic. In meeting. Told you not to come. I'm fine. Talk tomorrow. And so I sat on the tryst-laden bed and learned my lines.

DANISH WOMAN: Oh my... God!

THE STRANGER: Please. Please.

DANISH WOMAN: God!

THE STRANGER: I am man. Just man.

DANISH WOMAN: Don't come near me! Stay there! What... what *are* you?

I turned on the television, thinking it might help me sleep. Korean studio shows—chucklefests, game shows, news channels full of strobing hangeul, videos of camo-clad border soldiers, Kim Jong Eun, missiles. I looked again at the trickle of Johan's messages, and pressed the phone icon. It bleeped as it rang. Bleeeep. Bleeeep. The anchor continued to dispense his script. Bleeeep. When it answered, the voices were muffled, and not close to the mic. I couldn't make out any of the words.

Johan pirouettes on one sneaker, and stumble-falls into the glitter table, sending empty soju glasses onto their sides. He lands on top of the arm-folded girl, laughing, and Kim Dae Woo ruffles his hair, makes a Korean exclamation, shrug-grins at me. The arm-folder isn't sure whether to be victorious or furious, and settles for a sulk, pushing him off. What does it say in my film Kim sonsaengnim? he says. About three eleven a.m.?

Ah, Kim Dae Woo says, nodding, eyelids closing, opening, closing. Says is *magic* time. Yeah. Magic time. He turns to me. You—ah, you have seen yet, no?

Yes, I say.

Yes no?

No yes, I say.

She's seen it, Johan says, tugging himself upright, head-last. Of course she has. She's the boss around here aren't you? He looks at me, and I look at him, and I see all the topsy-turvy elements of the past five years of life, drunk and slumped

41

back into a vinyl noraebang booth, slit-eyeing me, and the arm-folder and the other one eyeing me too, seeming to, in some way, shift their understanding.

No, I say. No, I'm not a boss. I'm just a wife.

I'd woken on top of the love motel covers, to the unfurling spiel of the news anchor metamorphosing from dreamscore back into identifiably foreign language. It had been there, leading my subconscious brain down strange alleyways, sounds becoming other sounds, and then I was back in the room, the light of an overcast Yellow Sea morning and the throaty call of a streetside crab vendor drifting through the windows. One unchecked message from Johan sent at 3:09am: an imoji of a winking cat.

I showered, lathering myself in sachet shower gel, sachet shampoo, my own conditioner (an actress's hair is a precious commodity—I claim back the expense on my tax return). I stared at myself in the mirror: my ageing body, the rings forming under my eyes, deepened by sleeplessness.

The film festival was already half-over. The biggest in Asia: Japanese samurai westerns, Chinese political thrillers, Kazakh one-shot-wonders, Bong Joon Ho. Centum City, the festival epicentre: a futuristic Lego box of rhomboid halls and sloping rooves, all dull silver, soaking up the rain that had begun to fall, streaming down forty-five-degree glass walls—a typhoon was rumoured to be crossing the water from Japan. Festival-goers crowded in doorways, sheltered in the Central Building's atrium, passes hanging around their necks, soggy brochures in hand. The young man behind the desk in the ticket centre had horn-rimmed glasses, and cats on his shirt. Hello, can I help you?

I need one ticket for The Moon Also Rises, this afternoon.

Okay... he shifted the wheel of his mouse, said something in Korean to the girl behind him, who glanced up. Ah, this is the director Q&A screening.

That's right.

I'm afraid it's sold out. There's another screening tomorrow at ten fifteen in the CGV cinema in Gwangali that still has tickets available or there's another—

No, I need a ticked for the Q&A.

The girl spoke in Korean, eyes on me. Hello, I said. She quieted.

Yeah, these are popular events, they often sell-out. His shirt, buttoned to the collar, was fitted to his slender frame, shaped around his pectorals. The cats were in four or five repeating poses. One was winking.

How about the whole day pass, that gets me into anything, right?

You still need to get tickets for the events you wanna see, and this one is... sold out.

The whole week pass then.

Same thing.

A duo of overweight Chinese were queuing behind me, and the girl was now muttering to another colleague with open hostility.

Look, I said, I just need to get into that event, okay? Please.

I've come from Denmark. What can I do?

He looked down at his computer, at his hands, which, like the rest of him, were neat and clean, and for a moment, just a moment, I was sure he was going to help me.

You can get a ticket for the screening of Wild Jasmine at one forty-five this afternoon in the Central Building, screen three. That also has a director Q&A.

I could have told him I was the director's wife. I could have told him the director was a recovering drug addict, and that he was falling off the wagon, that he'd been away touring the festival circuit for three months and had stopped writing. I could have told him that. The girl, I was just noticing, had burn scars on the backs of her hands, little pale circles, where cigarettes had been driven in.

What if someone doesn't show?

If you wait until ten minutes into the screening, if there's a spare seat, they might let you in. But they might not.

The rain had eased somewhat. The streets were full, the subway floor patterned in murky hieroglyphs. I wandered the fish market, letting the sour, salty sea stench fill my nostrils. What was it Johan had said, just after we'd got married? Something about letting me down. I'll try not to let you down, or words to that effect, but he'd said it three times, at least. Before the wedding, and in his speech, that he made in the coastal restaurant in Bornholm to the six friends and no family members we'd invited, and then again, in Tisvildeleje on the camping trip we'd called a honeymoon. I'll try not to let you down, he'd said—yes, almost exactly that, and it had leapt out at me, the third time he'd said it, and a part of me had known that when men say these things to you they're not self-deprecations or gentle love affirmations, but warnings. Moments when they tell you, obliquely, couched in context, what they're going to do to you, so that you can never say you weren't told.

He'd been a perfect gentleman when we'd met, more or less—a perfect ex-junkie gentleman, with black nail polish on his fingernails, and black spacers making daylight in his ears. Try resisting that. This voice that came back to you from the other side of life and death, gentle as a father's. Hairs around his Adam's apple, below his stubble, where his shaving stopped. He'd tried everything, he told me, before he got to heroin— weed, speed, coke, ecstasy, meth, crack, barbiturates, nitrous, vicodin, valium, ketamin, everything except the hallucinogens. With the shit that's in my head? he'd said, and laughed, that big real laugh, with the smile that creased his cheeks and filled his face in such a way to make you feel everything must be okay, really, deep down. With such honesty, such humour, such a clear good nature. That surely makes everything okay. He still smoked weed, drank vodka straight, in big worrying gulps. I asked him to stop the weed—and he did, more or less, at first. He started using ginger ale, and sipping, but I'd notice how, after the moments when I'd stopped paying attention, his glasses would seem so much emptier.

The fish market was a tumult. Wet-handed vendors shouting across stalls, reams of wandering tourists and customers, Chinese, western, slowing and photographing, and local customers pushing between, delivery boys and women carving routes through the crowd, with wheeled flip-carts that threatened to cut off your toes if you got in the way. Styrofoam crates of octopi, gelatinously pulping in inches of water, sea cucumbers like monstrous penises, rockfish, bottom crawlers, sea snails. Life, if you'll excuse me, can be defined in the following manner: you don't know something's upon you until it's upon you. One minute I was rehearsing what I'd say after the Q&A, once he'd seen me there, in his crowd, his wife, and imagining what he might say to me, and the next my insides were trying to strangle me, and the octopi were on the floor. I noticed, some minutes later, sitting wet—bottomed on an upturned bucket next to the annoyed-concerned stall-owner's cubby, two working grandmothers speaking reassuring Korean at me, that it was raining again.

DANISH WOMAN: You're hideous.

THE STRANGER: It's just flesh. You could touch it, if you want.

DANISH WOMAN: Ugh! Fat chance!

THE STRANGER: But... would you? Would you touch me? Please?

DANISH WOMAN: No! No—stay back! Help!

THE STRANGER: I'm not—

DANISH WOMAN: HELP!

It's three shots of soju, back-to-back, that precipitate the vomiting. First, Kim Dae Woo pours a round to break the tension. Johan throws his back, eyes fixed on me, and the girls and Kim Dae Woo follow suit. I leave mine untouched. Johan eyes it, brim-full. Come on, don't be so boring. You're *here*, after I told you not to come— Kim Dae Woo tries to interject, but Johan won't be stopped, waves him silent, and girl #2 mutters something to the arm folder, and the arm folder giggles, and Johan picks up my shot and gulps it down. Oooh! they go. I will myself not to well up. More, J says, banging the table. My glass, which he'd emptied, falls on its side and describes an arc. I feel the years rushing to my brim. All the terribly, awfully loving moments we've shared. How he'd told me I was the only one he'd ever really made love with. How his whole body had shaken when he told me what was done to him when he was a boy, the pain he still felt sometimes, the years he'd been unable to keep an erection. The way he'd taken me by the hand and run me across the road, laughing, on our second day together, how he'd sung to the Chilli Peppers at the top of his lungs as we unpacked in the kitchen on my parents' pension in Hornbæk, booty bumping and twisting and slapping an air bass and play-grinding against my hip. How we'd built a bonfire on New Year's Eve, that same trip, out in the freeze, snow falling over everything like kisses. Johan throws his new shot back, the girls follow suit, Kim Dae Woo not far behind, and I fail to prevent the tears. He reaches for my shot, and I see his diaphragm convulse, his shoulders hunch, and out comes the rice-gruel, and soju, all over the

47

glitter-grain.

The cinema was back in Haeundae, a subway ride from Centum City, a ten-minute walk from the beach. The rain had become a storm—strobing over the waterlogged streets. Girls in blouses laugh-screaming, running, newspapers over heads, umbrellas turned inside out. I had no umbrella, no newspaper, so I simply ran, soaking and sweating in the humidity all the way. In the seventh floor lobby I dripped onto the glistening floor. Yellow warning signs displayed images of tumbling people.

There was a poster on the wall. An orange moon, a mysterious nighttime scene, a distant couple embracing or fighting—purposefully ambiguous. *the moon also rises* all in lower case, artisinal font, and *a film by johan beck*. I stood there staring at it, unable to look away, as I once had stood and stared at Van Gogh's self-portrait in the Chicago Art Institute, his broken, worn, vulnerable face, life-size on the wall, turned to hide the maimed ear, looking back at me. I'd just stood there, communing with him, for ten or twenty minutes, maybe thirty. I was twenty-one, twenty-two, and I had never been loved, not by anybody. I stood and communed with Johan's poster the same way, for five minutes, ten. Crowds were forming, queuing, waiting, funnelling in, for a Ken Watanabe epic, an Irish animation, and for Johan's film. *johan beck. a film by johan beck. the moon also rises...* I waited until the lobby was empty of all but a few wanderers and stragglers. At the entrance to the corridor that housed the different screening rooms stood a gangly young man in a red and black uniform, looking over a printed list on a clipboard, speaking into a walkie-talkie.

Excuse me—

He held up a finger. A voice crackled through. He answered it, looked at me. Yes?

I want to see The Moon Also Rises.

Ticket? he said, eyes on his clipboard.

I don't have one.

He made a kind of blank/sad face.

Oh, it's sold out, so...

Yes, they told me if I waited until ten minutes after it started that maybe I could just go in and find an empty seat.

But I think it's full, so...

A voice crackled through. He answered, turning away from me.

I don't mind sitting on the floor. Or standing, Really. I mean, I know it might be—

He held a hand to silence me, continued the conversation. I could hear string music, the raised voice of the mutual friend Johan had cast as the lead. A boy was sitting on a nearby window sill, kicking the carpet with his sneaker, a city mountain rising behind him. I waited for the conversation to finish.

I know it might be against your regulations or something—

I think it's full, he said.

Listen. I've come from Denmark and I need to be in that screening. So I'm going to go in and see if there is a spare seat—

I can't let you do that.

—and if there is I'm going to sit in it—

I can't let you do that.

—and if there isn't I'm going to stand against the wall, and if you don't like that you can fucking well *drag me out.*

Ah— I can't let—

Then stop me.

The boy in the window was watching, I knew, but I didn't turn back.

The screening room door opened into a world of my husband's making. There was a struggle going on, wrestling over a car door. As the screen revealed itself, an unseen man slammed the door on another man's hand.

Aaaaaaghhh

The auditorium was packed, brim-full. I saw a seat against the wall, scooched and ducked past tucked up knees, over handbags. Our mutual friend was busy kicking someone's teeth in. The gangly boy and an older woman appeared in the aisle, scanning the crowd. I sat tall in my seat, eyes on our mutual friend.

DANISH WOMAN: Get away from me, I'm warning you!

THE STRANGER: I'm not dangerous—

DANISH WOMAN: Back! Stay back! HELP ME! HELP!

THE STRANGER: I only—

DANISH WOMAN: <picking up knife> I'll kill you, do you hear me? You... monster! If you touch me, I'll kill you!

I had seen a rough cut, with temp sound, on a laptop in our apartment in Nyholm. A crepuscular crime drama that evolved across two eras, tracing the character's battle to escape violence and embrace love, doomed to fail. It was very good, and I told him so. Beautiful often, and (maybe more impressive for a first feature) undeniably proficient. And then there it was, twenty-feet tall and forty-feet wide, and weaved from the threads of a heart that lived half within me. The reluctant detective, pulled into darkness towards the truth, battling his own heart, seeking vengeance, destroying all hope. On a cliff near Hornbæk, not far from the beach next to my parents' pension, painted in noxious hues, he rides his scooter over the edge, smashes on the rocks—or is it in his head? In the previous scene, he'd smashed a villain's face in with a ball peen hammer.

The lights came up. Staff fussed in the wings. Cordless microphones were tested. A festival organiser addressed the crowd in a mixture of Korean and English. And then, to polite applause, my husband, who it seemed had been there a while, was introduced. He shuffled in his Converse and a distressed blazer (new), black sweater (a Christmas present from me). His eyes, quite often his giveaway, made small and deep-set by stress, were bright—he comes alive with crowds. He thanked us, and rubbed the stubble of his neck. He told us the film had been gestating inside him for ten years, more, ever since he started acting, and the festival organiser underscored him with a stream of translation. He told us the production, like any indie production, was a challenge—

that there was limited time, limited budget, ambitious plans, technical limitations, but the enthusiasm and commitment of the crew pulled everyone together. He told us, with the slightest hint of discomfort, that the film was very personal, that it's strange—but very satisfying, he quickly added—to be seeing it projected to audiences on the big screen, and then he made a self-deprecating joke, drew a good laugh. My husband is a charming man—it's how he hides his damage. He fielded questions. A Korean woman, via the festival organiser's translation, asked about the character of the young girl, her significance. A man, in good English, enquired about the music. It was during a question about how the film had been received so far that he saw me. The questioner, a few rows in front, had drawn his eye my way. I saw the reaction in his brow. One might expect my heart to have jumped at that moment, but he is my husband, and it did not jump. He huffed a laugh-like thing, shook his head, and refocused on the question. As it finished, I raised my hand, and the host looked my way. The film is very personal, I said. I felt a welling up begin. I managed to keep it at bay. It's very personal, so-- it must then be stressful to exhibit it publicly. Has that been difficult for you? He looked at me blankly for a moment, my husband. We hadn't shared a bed for three months, barely shared a word for two. I thought, for a moment, he was going to walk off the stage. But instead he sniffed, half-turned, back into professional mode, directed his avoidant answer mostly to the front few rows, glancing, now and again, at a spot just behind me.

I leave Kim Dae Woo to deal with the rice-gruel. The noraebang is on a basement floor, and as I take the stairs up to ground level, knees shaking, I find the typhoon. It is 3:11am.

Walking into it, I am lifted half-off my feet. The few people and cars still on the streets look in mortal danger. I can see the dark mass of the sea, in a fit.

He appears, pale and pink under the glow of the noraebang sign, supporting himself with a hand on the wall. Making it to the top stair he's knocked half-over by the gale. He screws his face.

When are you leaving? he yells.

Tomorrow, I yell. Filming starts on Tuesday.

The short, he yells, nodding, a tremor of nausea crossing his mouth.

We stay there a moment, in the tumult, as something not that distant creaks and falls.

DANISH WOMAN: You are despicable, do you hear me? You're... you're dis*gus*ting! I'd kill you right now, I would! How *dare* you think... go! Go, no, before I cut your guts open, do you hear me monster? Go! You MONSTER! You FREAK! Go!

I wake up on top of the sheets in the love motel. My flight is in four and a half hours. Johan stirs next to me. What are we going to do? he says, eventually, when my packing has woken him. I don't know. Answer me something, I say, sitting down. Have you slept with anyone else on this trip? He says no, and I almost believe him. I want to believe him. Outside, the crabseller is hawking his wares. I have a plane to catch, and a role to play.

I AM JUST a boy. I throw my net. Sticklebacks slip through the holes. My town is dark, my mother cold—it's winter now. Here, have my blanket! But she grumps. She breaks a cup, smashes the plates. The shadows come at night.

Men arrive, with hunting bags. So you're the little man, one says, the one with the teeth, the big stone ones, with the hairs on his neck and up his cheeks. They make themselves at home, and mother isn't cold so much no more. Go play somewhere else! Stone Teeth takes me out to shoot. Hold it to your shoulder, there, like this. It's going to kick. But guns don't have legs. I'm flying through the air. He's looking down at me. I heard your dad's due back tomorrow.

Dad looks familiar. He gets the watery eyes. The men are watching as he hugs me. Whad're you doing here? You know that don't you. You can tell an argument's coming, so I throw my ball as high as I can, Look at me! Look! I throw it up so it rolls down the roof and drops. Look! Throw it up so it drops, but it gets stuck in the guttering and the rifles make a sound like a mountain giant trying to scream. Mother says I'll be better off at fake aunt Ginette's. I'm not your mother no more, got it? I wave to her as she rides off on the back of Stone Teeth's motorbike, but she doesn't wave back.

I'm a boy in man's clothing. I kick the kid's teeth in. They lock me up again. When are you gonna learn? Old fake aunt Ginette shows up. I don't know what to do anymore, she says. How about get me out of here? No, I don't think so. Not anymore. I think you're on your own now.

The job pays shit, but it comes with a room—a windowless box above the repair shop. Slop the floors, clean the shitter and spitshine every car that comes in, and if you turn out not to be a blithering moron maybe I'll let you change the odd transmission. Big if! There's a girl, behind the counter in the lunchroom across the way, by the reservoir. She looks like she has a smile for everyone, but how it disappears when no-one's looking. You come in here a lot, she says. You work at the repair shop? In the dream, she's a seahorse, bobbing in the current, and behind a moon-sized shadow becoming a shark.

A voice makes the hairs stand on end, so I wash the toilet water from my hands and go take a look. There's a black sedan up on the rack, Phil half under it and yelling something about the transmission, and the boss nodding and listening to a man with hair down his neck and mouth full of giant stone teeth.

Should I kill him now? I ask the moon. Or wait? The moon's answers can't be heard, but that doesn't mean they're not there. I sit on the floor, next to Phil, as he fiddles around. Who is this guy anyway, he says, some big cheese? Got me. Hey! You two! If you scratch that sedan I'll cut your balls off and stuff them in your mouths—each other's mouths, got that? Who is this guy Boss? He looks at me, and retreats back to his office.

I wait for him to come again—he comes alone, checks the car. Seems okay, he says, with a voice that makes my stomach shake.

It's going to kick

I'm there with Phil, hanging back. Nice car, I say. Boss shoots me the ball-cutting-mouth-stuffing look. Stone Teeth sucks the last life from his Pall Mall. Wanna try it?

You can't believe how the air screams by, soundless, like the car's a fish through water, knife through butter. It's pretty smooth huh, he says. Sure, I say. Ha! Driven smoother have you? He eyes me. How much's Torven paying you? Room and board, I say. Room and board! That stingy old shit! So how you like being a slave? I eye him for a moment. The road is spooling out in front of us. The cliff is right there. A spasm of the elbow and over we'd shunt, off we'd tumble, down to a watery. That's my place up ahead. Bring it in, you can see how the other half live. An isolated remodelled farmhouse. A henchman sitting on the bonnet of an off-roader, eyeing me. How would you like to come and work for me?

Mister Pedersen offered me a job, I say. *What*? I let you go off on a joyride with a customer and you stab me in the back! Relax, I don't want it. Don't *want* it?! You're planning to turn down Søren Pedersen? Are you *trying* to get me killed? I let the day take me to the reservoir, the lunch room. Her hair is up in a bun, a net. Little strands slip through the holes.

Hey—what's your name anyway? She tells me, and I wonder why I waited this long to ask. We walk by the water. It's so huge, she says. You know how deep it is? Deep enough you could stack two skyscrapers top to bottom and still not touch the bed. Can you even imagine? In the water, the moon is split into ripples. I'm leaving town tomorrow, I say. Come with me?

I can't find the key for Phil's moped, but it isn't hard to get started—a tug and a splicing of wires. The cliffside road is empty as a dream, the moon approaching full, and hanging fat over the water like it thinks it's a sun. The two ball peen hammers, strapped to my sides, bump and jolt. I pull up a hundred yards away, walk the last. The house is cast in darkness, a couple of dimly glowing windows. The back door leads into the kitchen—I can see the henchman at the table. I grip hammer #1, turn door handle, squeeze hammer-grip—but henchman's passed out, drooling on hand, next to a half-empty bottle of Zubrowka.

I softfoot through the ground-floor, carpets you'd happily roll around on. He's up there, Stone Teeth, I can feel him. I hear a voice, feet. This is it. Squeeze grips #1 and #2, ready to pull—

Hey. You're nyuh— new. You're new. Right?

A moon-eyed, red-ringed spectre, forty looking fifty, swaying in the gloom, tumbler of vodka. She sways too far to one side, almost falls. Mother.

Hey. Kid. What the hell? Stone Teeth at the head of the

stairs. I'll need a place to stay. If I take the job. Mm, he grunts. Stig'll get you set up. You can start in the morning.

When morning comes, she's still swaying. Eyes of the moon. You remind me of someone, she says, looking far beyond me. I have one of those faces, I say. She scuffs around the house, nagging the henchman. I'd get rid of her, Stone Teeth tells me, but fuck it, I guess I love the old bird. Plus she still knows how to keep a man happy, if you know what I mean, and he digs an elbow into my ribs. I clean out his cellar, I weed the weeds. I rake the path and spitshine the henchman's off-roader. Try not to pull a muscle, she calls from the porch hammock and chuckles a familiar throaty chuckle that I remember from somewhere in my bones. I'm a child, just a child. All I want is for her to love me. Precious baby, precious thing, and she holds me to her bosom. Little baby, hey I just cleaned that you little shit, don't look at me like that—get away from me, why are you crying? Ha! Tears? Ha! Throaty chuckle. Stone Teeth has a meeting, two Albanians. I hear import-export talk, shipments, dockets. Hey, kid. C'mere. He offers me a drink, the house empty, my mother spectre passed out on the couch. You know who they were? I shake my head. Good. Stick with me kid, and you won't be raking leaves all your life, you get me? There are big things afoot.

I get a message to the lunchroom girl. Things got delayed— give me a week—I'll take you anywhere you wanna go. I give her no way to respond.

The moon is so huge it doesn't seem real. It's a perigree something something, Stone Teeth says. Biggest it'll ever be, they said on the news. Fuckin beautiful you ask me. I look at him: giant nostrils, broad face, hair up his cheeks, down his neck. Makes sense anyway cause tonight's a big fuckin night. A ghostly white car approaches on the cliff road. They're here. Go get Stig.

I stay on the fringes as the deal is done. Several bags full of mysterious product. Bag after bag. The Albanian brothers fill their car—opening hidden panels, secret spaces, filling them up, every nook and cranny. Mother Spectre appears next to me. She's staring, moon-eyed. Don't think I don't know, she hisses. Know what? I know who you are. My blood turns to water. My veins turn to paper. I know why you're *here*. You're nothing but a God-- damned— *spy*! and she whips my jacket open, exposing the hammers. I clamp a hand over her mouth, her breath hot and wet on my palm, yank her arm behind her back. Ggmhelmp! GgmHELMP! I don't have time for this. I hurl her into the old coop, tie a rag around her mouth. You know who I am? Do you? Look at me. Look. Go on. Her moons seem to clear. Look at me! Her brow contorts. She says my name into the rag, at least I think she does, but the rag eats it up. The ghost car is halfway up the drive. Stig and Stone Teeth are counting the stacks of money, feeding them through an electric counter, *ttthhhrap, ttthhhrap*. Hey kid. Get a load of this. Ever see anything like this? I haven't, it's true. I have two hammers strapped to my back, a hundred grand in front of me, and my mother's specture gagged in a hen coop. I smash Stig's teeth in, but the heart has already gone out of me. Wha— what— My name is Aksel. You killed my father, and you stole my mother. A cloud crosses over his face. I know who you are kid. And I didn't steal your mother—he stole her from me. And I didn't force her to come back. And— he takes a step forward, deep into hammer range— your pop ain't dead. Get my drift?

The road back to town is 2am dead. The cliff is on the other side now. A spasm of the other elbow, and down I'd go to my watery. So that's what I do—I shunt to my right, tumble tumble, smash the scooter on the rocks, disappear into the night. At least, that's how it seems. Or maybe I go back to the reservoir, and go scuba diving with the girl, build a home in the deep. Or maybe I go back to Phil and the Boss, share a crate of Carlsberg and laugh laugh laugh. Or maybe I age, wake up in Stockholm with a Swedish wife. Who is this woman? Round chinned and dark, huffing in her sleep, she asks me to check on the boy. The apartment is chilly, dim—a siren passing somewhere nearby. This moon-headed boy is twisted in his crib, head all the way over and body limp as if he's been broken, but his little chest HUFFS as a diver pulled to the surface and re-engaging his lungs. His miniscule fingernails, so small it's like a joke. I'm old— can feel it—but a boy—that too—I take him in my arms, just to try. Warm squirming thing. I see a ghost in the mirror, a moon-eyed spectre, holding his child. The wife's voice is calling to me. Morning should arrive soon, but dark it will be—it's still winter. I hold onto him, for a little longer.

HE'D MASTERED

the fall, the roll, the headbutt recoil, the plunge of death, it was just the yank that spooked him: braced around the belly, the Teenage Actress would roundhouse to his chest, the wire would taughten, and he'd be pulled back and up as if by a storm wind or the hand of a deity, to smash backwards into a strategically placed pre-weakened fake wall or plate of sugar glass. The smash was no problem — it was the yank. Maybe I could help you practice, the Teenage Actress had said. Her trailer was messy, and he noticed drifts under her eyes, that her stage make-up must usually have covered up. She kicked him again and again, but it was no use. Without the wire it's not the same, he told her. Well, she said, I could open the door of the trailer and you could stand in front of it? Thanks, he said, but it really needs the wire. She seemed to understand. Mind if I change? She made to remove some clothes, and so he excused himself. He was a gentleman stuntman.

He tried practicing with a length of wire tied around his midriff, and his roommate tugging on cue. You have to really pull, he'd said. The roommate expressed a lack of confidence, and so it proved. Confidence is so important.

He tried with a length of rope attached to the rear of

Jimmie's Honda Civic. On three! he'd yelled. Jimmie gunned it, but it was more of a drag. Wish I could help ya bro, Jimmie'd said.

He decided the only way was to practice for real. He broke into the studio, only to find the Teenage Actress sitting on the prop settee in character. No words were exchanged, but the situation was understood. She watched as he strapped himself in. Do me a favour, he said, and score me out of ten? She was as good as her word. When he met her on another set several months later, their bond was implicit. It's hard to overstate the value of a confidant.

THERE WAS a corpse—but there

usually is, isn't there. Isn't there? Yes, for sure—always.
You can't move for sodding corpses. Corpses that float to the
surface, mouth-pooted, eyes-slitted, corpses glimpsed because
disembowelled, dismembered, corpses of boys, girls, women,
corpses of men—don't forget the corpses of men. Corpses
on slabs frost-dotted, morgued; corpses stacked in piles by
roadsides; corpses fresh-slaughtered that the embattled hero
must clamber over; corpses found falling from closets; attic
corpses, stuffed in storage. There are corpses that reanimate,
corpses whose eyes flash as they change, corpses that come
roaring back, the angry dead, plague-like, noveau locusts;
corpses that creep, corpses that spring, slow death/fast death,
dread vs panic. Corpses discovered in the closing movement,
revealing truths; corpses that fill the opening frame, posing
questions. There's always a bloody corpse. This one was
rubber.

Realistic job they've done, I said, and gave it a poke.

Ow!

Not rubber then.

I was a retired fisherman. I'd grown tired of the inscrutable
ocean and retired to my cottage to brood. And then: corpse.

Not quite opening frame. The irascible woman playing my wife said

Is that how you're going to do it?

She was talking about my read-through.

Well. Yes, I said. But more.

How much more? she said. I was starting to become attracted to her.

Just the right amount, I said, hint of a wink. I've always been powerless to resist women who can't stand my breathing guts. It's my only major character flaw. She sighed a sigh intended to signal idiocy.

Look, she said, her silvery hair leaf-like in the half-light, I'm hiding something, right? She smelled of her set clothes and the aubergines she'd had for lunch. And you know that, and you're trying to get it out of me, and boom! Corpse. She doffed the rolled up script on her open palm at the boom. I don't think you're going to be so... *cred*ulous. Right?

I tire of people telling me how to act, so these days I tend to agree and then just do whatever I feel like, which not only avoids tiresome conversations but has the added bonus of annoying the snot out of people. Oddly, I do enjoy annoying the snot out of women I'm interested in going to bed with. I find it an inexplicably successful strategy. Something about the kinds of women I'm attracted to compels them to want to solve me, like a tourist unable to sleep until they've found the mosquito buzzing around their bed and firmly swatted it, and for the purposes of this analogy I quite enjoy a good swatting.

I think, our corpse said, sitting up—

Shush! she said, You don't get a say.

I felt it was time to nip this in the bud. Fine, I said, you're quite right. Credulity isn't the thing. Not for this scene. No, what this scene needs is...

*In*credulity?

Precisely.

I was actually going to say that., said our corpse. That was exactly what I was going to say.

I tricked her into coming for a stroll with me by pretending I didn't want her to. An oldie but a goodie, much like myself. The coast path was atmospheric in the gloam: shadowy gorse and a clifftop tumble to the gush and regush of the massing sea. Not exactly a classic this show is it, I said finally, when I felt my silence had become suitably magnetic. Not exactly, no, she said, but at our age one doesn't get the luxury of being picky. Not often at any rate. I used to get piles of scripts, always something interesting buried in the slush. Now I'm lucky if there's slush. That's life, I said, which didn't help anyone, but had the advantage of making me sound carefree. Well obviously, she said. But that doesn't make it any more pleasant does it. I stopped then, and looked out to sea. In the darkness, you couldn't quite tell what was out there. Some shifting pattern, as if from a quilt, not quite discernible to human eyes. I passed this thought on to her, and she looked at me strangely. Look, I said, life's roughly as pleasant as you allow it to be. She sort of snorted, but there was a look in her eyes, and so I slid a hand around the back of her neck as if to

67

kiss her, felt her soften rather than stiffen, the warm softness of her neck against my palm. I held my eyes on hers. What are you doing? she said quietly. I held a finger up to my lips. Shhh.

In this episode, the discovery of the corpse provokes a mystery. I, the retired fisherman, despite discovering the body, become suspect number one, and the expert, professional, emotionally isolated, eponymous detective from the mainland arrives to investigate. The actress playing her is know-her-when-you-see-her famous, and fresh from a couple decades of yoga and awards functions. She is lithe as a dancer and lined as a purse. I couldn't have done it, I tell her, how could I? One thing I've learned in my profession, she tells me, is that anyone is capable of anything. No! I say. I couldn't't've! How could I do that to my own son?

They skip ahead a few pages, and we squeeze in an exterior scene as the day's last traces of light evaporate, a scene from later, before my redemption, in which the detective doesn't like me one bit. My wife is nowhere to be seen. By nine we're back at the tiny hotel bar, by ten we've cleared it out, cast and crew vamoosed. Early start tomorrow? I ask her. When she was at the height of her fame, I'd order chicken and cashew nuts and watch her unravel mysteries. Not for me, she says, and takes a sip of her gin. I notice she hasn't bothered to add the tonic. Star's perk is it? I'd've thought you'd be needed all hours. They cut me the odd break, she says.

I slip onto the stool next to her, eye a group of local drinkers throwing looks our way from a corner—the only other patrons left. What do you get out of this show? I ask her. A bloody great paycheque, she says. And? A big fat starring credit. And? She''s half-turned to face me, perma-glare half-defrosted. The odd flirtatious co-star. She gives me an up-and-down look that's hard to misinterpret.

The ocean makes its music, knits its quilt, out beyond the blanket. Tell me something I wouldn't guess about you, she says. Alright, I say. I used to be a monk. No, really. Buddhist. I summered in Thailand all through my thirties. Our summer is their rainy season. Oh I think I knew that, she says. The rainy season bit, not the monk bit. Well, I'd go over in June, come back in September, sun-speckled and wrung out like tenderised pork, soft and smiling and ready. I had a buddhist girlfriend for a while. Quite a woman actually. I was... a bit of a mess if I'm honest. Not an honourable man. A bit... lost.

Well, you can ordain over there, whenever you like. Go to a temple, shave your head, your brows, don the robe. I ordained in a temple in Phrae—that's in the North. A forest temple. I'd wake at three, pray, chant, meditate, sweep the sala—that's where you pray—sweep the path. Eat one meal a day at 11—huge meal, that the locals would provide—they do it to earn merit you see. I planned to stay three months, the whole summer. Ended up staying until the following summer. I still speak a little Thai. Yahk ja poot dee gwah, der seeung soong seeung dtum yahk mahk. She looks at me

69

in a way I haven't been looked at in a long time. You are full of surprises, she says, and the light is casting shadows on her shallow folds, on the sheets. I think that might be nicest thing I've had said to me for many a year.

Our corpse is ready to go: so ready he's impatient. My make-up's going to smudge under these lights, he's saying, can we get a move on? Can we get a move on! I yell. Our cadaver is getting impatient! He gives me the 'alright smartarse' eyes. He's not so bad, as corpses go.

We play the scene straight, not for laughs. The second corpse of the episode, and this one seems to be the icing on the cake. Alright, I say, alright. I hated his stinking guts. He killed my son, I know he did—even if not by his hand, he drove him to it. But I'm no killer! She, the detective, seems to believe me. I'm not sure if she's meant to—if her character's meant to—find I can't quite remember the script. But the lines find their way out, and I find my way into her driver's car, and the lines and walls and people of the location fall away behind us.

Only, it isn't her car—it's my wife's. The woman playing my wife's. A thick and heavy silence, scored by the soft thrum of the German engine. So that's your last day is it? she says finally, working her fingers in her lap, the driver silent in front. 'Fraid so. You'll have to muddle on without me. I see, she says, bitterness falling into her voice. No—that wasn't... I didn't mean it like that. But it's too late—she's gazing out at the black quilt. I think you'll find I'm quite adept at 'muddling along.'

I didn't mean that, I say. Putting a hand on her skirted knee. She allows it, remains staring out at the patterns in the darkness. There's always a corpse isn't there, she says eventually. At least one, I say. And the journey seems alright then: the German engine, my hand on her knee, the two of us gazing into darkness.

SHE HAS a layer around every organ: lungs, liver, kidneys, heart. A layer thin as sugar glass. The way its explained, it's some freak keratin mutation, like having fingernail one-cell thick and brittle as ground-frost encircling all her crucial parts. It means the organs are extremely delicate, the doctor told her. Beneath the keratin layer — well, think of if you took off all your finger- and toe-nails. So. If this layer ruptures at all, even slightly, we're gonna be in serious trouble.

She comports herself with grace, because if she doesn't, she will crack and liquefy. Over-exertion — I'm talking even a coughing fit, the doctor said — could cause internal haemorrhaging. She will float through this world, she decides, until such a time as she cracks, and then she will let go of solidity with grace, let go of painlessness with grace, and embrace liquefaction. Knowing it, that she is due to be cracked at any point, makes things easier, in a way. She finds a taste for war films. She watches and watches on the sofa, in bed, in the soft spaces her mother urges her not to leave. Your problem, an effective soldier tells an ineffective one, is that you think you've still got a chance of making it out alive, but Blythe — the effective soldier leans in — your only hope is to accept that you're already dead. She writes this down in one of her notebooks. She knocks the glass off the coffee table. Its sound fills the room for a fraction of an instant, into which she pours herself, and in which she lives for a while, echoing around and around and around.

THE TEENAGE

Actress shows up in knee-highs and instantly regrets it. She shows up in a leather skirt and feels the jarring lilt of her hips as she walks down the sterile corridor to the room of men and women and clipboards. She shows up without having showered or washed her hair or brushed her teeth, greasy faced and gnarly, just like the character. She shows up with her hair up, down, cut, dyed, she shows up half an hour after a crying fit, shows up hungover from the director's brother's house party. She stabs daggers into her eyes, metaphorically, for their consideration, and is told she'll hear back only if she's been successful because they're seeing a lot of girls today and they don't have time to mollycoddle anyone who doesn't cut it.

Guess what, her manager says.

What? she says, and her manager looks disappointed. She realises she was meant to come up with some kind of quip.

Sigh. Well, kiddo, you got the show. Primary cast member, *if* it goes to series you're locked in for two years. *Don't. Fuck. This.*

The show involves a lot of high-kicking in mini-skirts. She defeats several evil hordes, with the help of the bookish wisecracker who can never seem to talk to girls, and her maternal aunt-slash-mentor. She builds up her muscle density and learns to roundhouse. A succession of extras and stunt-people go flying. Quite the power: crouch, twist, kick, the faintest of contacts and WHOOSH! Awaaaay they go! She doesn't like to go home if possible—her roommate might, she suspects, be poisoning her food. So she stays, wanders the empty darkened set, reading, writing, claiming to be practicing her lines. She trawls her bored-ass way through Baudelaire. He wasn't so hot. She drools for Thom Gunn, tries to replicate a few. She can't get the words right. She can't get anything right. Except when the camera is pointed on her, and it's time to stab her own eyes. Metaphorically. Or when a beefy gym body is placed in front of her with a wire attached. One night one of the beefs appears on the set. The nice one with the British accent. He asks for her help. She promises to do her best. And she does. She does her best for him. She sees him again a few months later, on the set of the psychological thriller.

THE SET is filled with smoke, great rolling bales of it, so thick the Stuntman can't see his mark. Before he knows it, a beam is hurtling towards him.

Jesus Chri—

That was one hell of a duck n' roll Buddy-O.

Well, y'know. Not my first hoe-down.

Right. Where you from, England?

Yup. Milton Keynes. I mean you won't know where that—

Stuart! We still need someone to play the cop?

The role comes with two lines—his first two lines. In the scene, the young but ambitious fashion designer's mental state has started to fracture, thanks to the machinations of her corporate embezzler husband. She has been hearing things, seeing strange people hanging around the apartment building. He has encouraged her to hide the burns on her arms, to up her meds, and nothing is what it seems. Her neighbour has been seen wielding a large knife—but maybe that was in her head, along with the bloody footprint in the corridor (it wasn't there when she looked again—although, mop marks?). An encounter in the storage room leads to a revelatory discovery, a pursuit down the fire escape, and that's where the cop comes in.

He sees her by the Kraft services, picking the sprinkles from a moon pie. She looks the same, but thinner, and emptier.

Hey there stranger, he says. He is surprised by how she jumps, and how, on recognising him, she seems to become uncomfortable.

Oh heeey. An acne trail by one corner of her mouth has been daubed with concealer. Fancy seein you ere guv'nor, she says in a terrible Dick Van Dyke brogue. She has the eyes of a scared rabbit.

Yeah, small town I guess. Hey, I think we've actually got a scene together.

Her brow contorts, just like her terrorised character's. Whaddyou mean?

He tells her about the beam, the duck n' roll. As they sit on the step of her trailer, her smoking, him drinking a fridge-cold protein drink, she seems to calm.

You're partying pretty hard huh, he says.

She laughs—if you can call it a laugh. Well what else is there to do?

He doesn't quite know how to read her. The straps of her top and the straps of her white bra diverge over her shoulders. Her nails are chewed, the hangnails bloody.

I've never had any lines before, he tells her.

Well shyeah, you're the kick-me-in-the-chest guy. You nervous?

He shrugs his mouth. Not really. I've done scarier things than this.

She smirks. Ooh, bad ass huh? Like what?

Well. Last train from Leighton Buzzard on a Friday night for starters.

He is smaller than the other stuntmen, narrower. She notices the bars of his collarbone, the speckled calves. She notices how he straightens his back when the other stuntmen arrive, tilts up his chest. She notices quite a lot about him.

Shoot day number thirteen and they're already behind schedule. Her husband, the corporate embezzler, has turned on the charm. It was raining cats and dogs outside, so she's soaked to the bone, but as she enters she finds he's lit candles, laid out the Egyptian rug. Fresh made aubergine parmesan is bubbling on the stove. You made my favourite? His sleeves are rolled up over his forearms, and he unbuttons his collar. Well it's our anniversary, sugar-pie. Our anniversary is the 27th, she says. He snort-laughs, straightens her sodden scarf. No, that was our first fuck, not our first date. Here, open the Pouilly-Fuisse. Her wet hands slip on the bottle. Just let me do it. Go get changed, I'm serving in five. Go on.

They make love on the rug to the strains of Billy Joel. He looks into her eyes just like he used to before they were married. She has a strip of flesh-coloured gusset covering her genitals, and the Billy Joel is theoretical. The lighting technician tells the director something in Danish. She hears him parse out some Danish curse. Helvede. Er du sikker?

79

The man playing her husband shifts his weight above her. She can smell his scent. Er—sorry, sorry guys, we need to, ah— også lysene? Yea, we need to reset. We'll take a break. Twenty minutes only everybody, please. Can we get the robes for Kristen and Jeremy please?

They disrobe again, a bigger, brighter light hanging over them, recommence the act. The act of love. She presses his body against hers, feels the warmth of his hairless back. When they're done, he tells her she needs to be ready to leave for 6am because the flight is at nine.

What flight?

What flight, he scoffs, as he fastens his wristwatch. To Houston, dummy.

He has told her about this several times, he reminds her. He shows her emails that he apparently sent her that she can't for the life of her remember reading. We've dis*cussed* this in *so* much detail Karen! He tells her she must have skipped her meds—but she hasn't, look, look at the blister pack, she's right up to date. She can't understand what's happening. He tells her he's calling doctor Fleischman to discuss upping her dosage.

They break for lunch. The Stuntman eats a cruller, and watches how she hides herself behind a moveable wall.

Then, although it means skipping ahead 18 script pages, it's their scene. She's running down the fire escape at a clip, bare feet slipping on the rain-slick bars. Four flights up the husband has gone Roy Batty psycho (or has he? Is it her?), and he's made it to the window—he leans out to roar her name before he spots her and clambers out (and isn't that what a concerned hubby would do?).

The mist is spooling, the cameraman, with his hovering, alien-like gimbal, bothering the space around her, and suddenly she's slipping, falling—

—landing in the arms of a policeman.

Whoa! Slow down there miss.

She gives away nothing—it's incredible. She is thoroughly her character—the nineteen-year-old veteran he has been thinking about at night when he closes his eyes has vanished. Now, there is this other young woman, and she is terrified to her bones, cat-eyeing him from a few inches away, and she's beautiful, under the terror, and older than her years, so much has happened to her, he can see in the lines of her face, *so* much has happened to her, and his hand is on the firm slick softness of her gymmed shoulder.

H—help me! Please! My— my husband! The man playing her husband bellows from above on cue. A sound man adjusts his boom mic.

Calm down ma'am, it's alright. Tell me the situation.

He feels he fluffed the vowel in calm—he thinks she thought so too, she seemed to flinch. In the following scene, he has not helped her, but delivered her back into the arms of her husband. It is written so that he has no lines, but he is there, and he gets to make an ambiguous gesture of possible conspiracy which only adds to her character's despair, and which the increasingly panicked Danish director makes him repeat more than a dozen times, until he wonders if basic assertiveness makes it necessary for him to tell the director to fuck off (he decides to err away from basic assertiveness and towards careerism).

He does see her again—in his pre-dream pageants, of course, before those thoughts have run their course, but on the set too. Not that day—that day she fled the set still in her character's tears and locked herself in her trailer, was still in there when the car service took him and two of the other stunt people away. But another day, the following week, the final week of the shoot. He has a scene in which, almost beside the point, he is killed, his body briefly discovered. The Danish director has been replaced by a second-unit director, a balding beach-tanned fifty-year-old Californian who has not bothered to learn his name and who he takes an instant dislike to. No-one on the set seems to have retained any interest in him whatsoever. It is as if he has been reduced to a status below that of a stuntman—just another nothing "actor", and not even a very handsome one. He sees her beforehand, as he is trying to mentally prepare himself, picking at her wristbands. She sees him seeing her too.

\sad hitmen\

TAKE Alain Delon. In a Citroen-grey trench coat, skirting Parisian byways, sifting through a hundred keys for the one that will start a stolen car, closed-mouthed, or lying in his bed, smoking, fully-clothed, before a job goes wrong. Or Clooney, gunsmithing, making love to a Scandinavian, assembling a rifle, meeting in an Italian café an unfamiliar contact, wandering the countryside, getting shot in the back. And not just hitmen: James Caan, cracking safes like a stoic; Jean Servais, kissing life goodbye the only way he knows how—with a heist; Ryan Gosling, gunning a Camaro and taking a knife in the gut in a magic hour parking lot. The sad expert; the root of man. Dedicated to the perfection of their skillsets and strict adherence to their (criminal) moral codes they walk the hinterlands, tool in hand, deaths on conscience, until they stumble across another desolate soul in female form (the subplot is always romantic, the expert always straight), open themselves to her, with all their stunted potential for love and compassion, until, finally, they're shot from behind. The sadness is a bittersweet smile: after all, he was damn good at his job.

\ *jean* \

AGAINST the odds, the German director casts her as Joan of Arc, when she has no experience whatsoever to speak of, only dreams, and the kind of large-eyed, smooth-skinned beauty of a girlchild. Later, she remembers being burned at the stake twice: once on set, under the monacular gaze of the German director's viewfinder and three dozen crew members, and once when the reviews came in. This is before FBI COINTEL of course—but in hindsight, incidents aren't always so easy to separate, timelines not always mono-directional.

She walks into the Parisian bedroom—location, no sets for these French directors—as a character she will later claim not to care for. A crop-haired breezy *Americain* in a narrative enamoured of national stereotypes and the definitions that separate men from women. She dozes in the bed with Jean-Paul—smooth-chested, Atlas-bodied, flat-nosed casuist Jean-Paul. She is a tool of collocation. In the twenty-three minutes of this shoot presented in cinemas, later on video, DVD, stream, she will become something not exactly timeless, but existing in a different designation of time to the one she walks through daily. People will say they have fallen in love with her—with what they see of her—of her as this character—in what is shown of this shoot. And this is still before FBI COINTEL—years before, though not many. David, her brother, of course, died in a car crash when he was eighteen. Francois, her husband, beat the shit out of her, before attempting to launch his directorial career with her, mid-estrangement, as his star. *La recreation.* Estrangement—a funny word. From the French—*estrangier*. Like the Camus. As if strangers is a state you can return to. Perhaps it is—a different you, a different pair of the pair of you, because it seems the past version will always be intimately acquainted with that past Francois, the one who was still just a lawyer, his celluloid ambitions discreet.

And then there was Romain, sweet Romain, who had his moments, but never beat the shit out of her. He saw the men who followed her, the cars parked outside their apartment. Heard that insectoid hum and *cli-click* when he picked up the phone. The story they fed to Newsweek, about the Black Panther fathering her baby, it fell straight from the meta-plan: 'cause her embarrassment and cheapen her image' says the memo, you can read it yourself. The story wasn't true of course—the baby, in fact, belonged to Carlos, the revolutionary who she'd has an affair with on the set of the Mexican civil war drama, but Romain, decent Romain, said it was his. She—said she was his. A little girl, born early, weighing 4lbs—a little tiny flickering speck of starlight. A few pulses of wooly lids over blurry retinas, a few days of earthly light. Like a match you strike that doesn't catch. On the day that Jean's body is found, decomposing in a blanket in the backseat of her Renault in the 16th arrondisement, her next of kin is an Algerian conman, who sold her apartment for eleven million francs so he could open a restaurant.

iii.

\ *re-education* \

THEY drained the land, and out came the worms. Great writhing masses of them, strings of coiled meat that they'd scoop out of the buckets, in gloved handfuls, just to see how they'd fall. They'd eat them too—squash and fry them up in garlic and oil. Go to Yunnan, they're a regional delicacy these days.

But the kids don't eat them. The young people I mean, father says.

Who knows what the kids do and who cares. I'm talking about tradition, says grandfather. You know about the camps? Nineteen fifty-eight and on for three, four years, through the great famine. There were camps full of academics, smelting pig iron like commoners. Re-education.

Mm.

Mm? That's what you have to say, mm? Imagine—a physics professor, maybe a dean, ploughing fields through winter until the food ran out, and then just wasting away to the bones and dropping dead, in some fucking converted grainhouse in Jiangxi province—I had friends who... anyway. What was I saying?

Worms.

Right. They drained the land and out came the worms.

I watch him, stuffing tobacco into the bell of his pipe. It curls into threads of smoke that reach up for the ceiling, and on the ceiling: ghosts.

Boy. Come, he says, and a boney hand creeps around my shoulder. Look up there. What do you see?

Smoke.

And? That shape there?

A... swordsman?

Ha. Good. There?

His friend?

Or his victim.

What's a victim?

His eyes brighten yellow with the bud as he sucks.

Xiaotong! Father is screaming again. The switch leaves welts all down my legs. He wants you to be strong, like him, says grandfather. Are you strong?

Yes.

Really? Try and take this coin from me.

I tug and tug and out it slips.

Ha. Very strong boy.

He kicks my shin.

Ow!

He retrieves the coin, puts it back in his pocket. Strength isn't everything, boy.

Xiaotong! Father is screaming. I stuffed the pillow with coal, to train my head for rocks, but it seems now to be black. Ruined! Switch. Idiot! Welts. If you learned to think before you act you wouldn't make your father so angry, says the mother woman. Sorry mother. Her arms stretch out of her sleeves. I tug on an earring. Ow! Smack. Her neck has lines. The ceiling ghosts are dancing again. Grandfather! He doesn't look at me—he knows I've been bad. He jogs little sister on his knee, lets her light his pipe, so I pinch her legs thirty times after lights out with a hand over her mouth until she stops whimpering. You're the victim—got that? Teary nod. Little welts.

Xiaotong! Father's beer over the table—smells like old bread. He fills himself up with warmth. Come, boy. Arm around, knee bounce. This one—squeeze and ear-tug—this one's going to be big and strong, aren't you? Yes sir. Ha! Okay, strong one, let's see. Fight your old man. Slaps and pokes, so I kick his knee. Pipe buds fire in his eyes, and grandfather watching as he puffs—I'm on the floor and vision flashing red. Smack. Looming over. Smack. Think you're tough! Huh? Go to your bed! Worm!

Were you re-educated? I ask grandfather.

Me? Ha! They couldn't have gotten me if they tried. Too famous, too powerful. In life, young one, you are only as strong as those you can defeat, and no stronger. Who do you want to decide your fate, you? Or someone else? The ghosts, above, are in caucus.

Me.

Right. He smiles a brown-toothed smile. Rotted down to nubs, and he smells of forests and dead plums—so different to the grandfather on the screen. How could he have let himself get so *old*? Mother woman is somewhere, laughing. Your father is strong, like I was. Maybe one day you'll be stronger than him. What do I have to do? I ask him, but he doesn't really answer, so I ask the ghosts, but they don't really answer either, not really, just take it as an invitation to creep down from the ceiling and make a circle around my bed, and we hum the ghost tune together, quietly, so no-one will hear. But sister does hear, and in she comes, with her 'you're humming again?', so I punish her, as she deserves, and which she accepts. Did you know people eat worms? I say to her, and she shakes her head. They squish and fry them and eat them all up, with mud rice made of mud, and then they either turn into worms or into ghosts, depending on how many they eat, and that's how some of the ghosts get to be ghosts, did you know that?

We watch one of grandfather's movies, in the cinema by the harbour. In this one, grandfather is younger than he usually is, and no-one in the movie can speak, but you can tell it's him. He falls in love with a servant girl, but her fiancee discovers, comes after him, chases him into the forest. Young grandfather twists his body like a scorpion. Six different men come and go flying before he faces off against the fiancee man.

Did he die? I ask father in the car home. The man grandfather was fighting? How should I know? he says. Mother woman is smoking one of her long cigarettes. There are ghosts, out beyond the windows, but these are solid— moaning as they tap the glass, pointing at their gummy mouth-holes. They want our souls, I tell little sister, and she gasps. Father will protect us, she says. I look at the back of father's square head and know he won't. I roll down the

92

window—the ghost man rocks back, leans in, finger-curled to open mouth— Ya! Xiaotong! What are you doing! I'm letting him get closer so I can kill him.

THE DANISH director egests the rice-gruel

and soju all over the glitter-grained table. His wife grabs her bag and leaves. Aish, Johan-nim, don't worry, don't worry. It's no problem, don't worry. The girls have skittered back away from the drips. They've seen it all before.

Kim Dae Woo watches as the owner fills a bin bag with vomit-sodden paper towels. He finds the Danish director sitting on the stairs that lead up and out to street level, head in hands, and behind him a raging typhoon. The wife appears to be gone.

Johan-nim! Let's get you home, huh?

He looks up at Kim Dae Woo, with a look of confusion. Home? he says.

Your hotel.

He calls the car service, tells the Danish director to stay right where he is, and back down in the basement lobby he finds her: the noraebang girl of his dreams. Girl—she must be thirty. She has the poise and scrupulous disposition of royalty. Her filtrum is perfect: the slightest upward tilt.

I have to take him back to his hotel, but I'll be back.

She huffs, ever so slightly. My shift finishes in a half an hour, she says.

He tells her she is under no circumstances to leave the establishment until he returns, at which point, he informs her, she will leave with him. He slips the owner twenty thousand won, instructs him to order some food. The owner accepts the money with a gracious bow.

The Danish director leans his head against the tinted window. The car interior is peaceful despite the storm, quiet, a gentle burble from the radio. Beyond the windows Busan is empty, under attack—as the car is exposed to the gale, now and again, it's shunted sidewards, rocking on its suspension. Apocalyptic rain strobes over everything like a spell.

Jeez, Kim Dae Woo says. Heavy huh. The Danish director murmurs something like agreement. When Kim Dae Woo had been living in New York, during his internship, he'd experienced a storm far worse than this: Hurricane Sandy. Gusts over a hundred miles per hour, fourteen-foot storm surge at Battery Park. He'd watched it from the twelfth floor Midtown office of the production company, with Sue, the twenty-two-year-old Korean American NYU graduate with whom he'd been having an affair. Working late, they'd got stuck for the night, raided the office fridge for leftover noodles and melon balls, picnicked on the carpet as the wind shook the floor-to-ceiling windows so hard two of them cracked. They'd thought genuinely they might explode, shower their affair with glass, so they retreated to the meeting room where he undressed her and had her on the floor by the flipchart he'd used earlier that afternoon to give a presentation on distribution norms in the Korean market. CJ Entertainment, he'd told them, owned a third of the cinemas in the country, so naturally their films tended to account for the biggest of big box office success stories, but it was important to remember that the Korean system required that 40% of all films screened in cinemas be domestic productions, and that it was this regulation that ensured the growth and development of the domestic film industry, not just domestically but on the international stage too. Bumping the leg of the flipchart with Sue's head he'd decided he was going to come inside her, and he did, and she slapped him in the face, he slapped her back, twice, just to establish who was in charge, before he remembered that she was basically American, and that was the end of that, not discounting a further seven or eight hours stuck in the office together with the windows cracking. The owner of the company, however, was Korean-Korean, and so it was Sue who wasn't there when the office reopened, spotless new windows where the cracked ones had been.

Opening the Danish director's door for him, as a gentleman would for a lady, the director falls almost flat on his face, has to be scooped up, and is soaked across his front. Rain driving, Kim Dae Woo shepherds him in through the automatic doors, into the hushed hotel lobby, trailing a slick of storm water. He slips the muttering night receptionist ten thousand won for the trouble, gets him into the elevator. Man, I thought you Danes could hold your drink, he says, chuckling, but the Danish director is staring at his own reflection in the elevator's mirror. When they get to his door, he says something in

Danish. Huh?

He draws in a lungful of air. I've destroyed everything.

His voice, his face, are so desolate that for a moment Kim Dae Woo is unable to respond.

Ha ha! Bullshit! You're about to become a *star* man! Your film is gonna be huge. I mean—indie huge, but that's still some serious huge—

Shht, he spits, hand on the closed door steadying himself. No. No. He shakes his head, but doesn't seem to have anything else to say.

Well, whatever you say, mister director sir, but I know my people are looking forward to a lucrative relationship with Europe's newest hot young filmmaker. As soon as he sobers up. He holds the keycard to the door. *Blee-leep*.

No, the Danish director says.

Alright, alright, in we go Johan-nim—

No!

He braces himself against the doorframe, swings his lazy head to face Kim Dae Woo.

I have to. I have... I have to go to my wife.

Kim Dae Woo sighs—he was afraid of this. It is already fifteen minutes since he left the noraebang, and the owner of the world's most perfect filtrum. She'll be there in the morning, Johan-nim, when your head is clearer, huh? She doesn't need to see—

But he is already reeling back down the hallway, towards the elevator, muttering firm declarations, the word wife.

After the firing of Sue, New York had begun so seem slightly nightmarish. He'd never thought of himself as the kind of man who would destroy a young girl's career trajectory for the sake of his penis, but he wasn't the kind to go against the flow either, certainly not when it was flowing in his favour. The walk from Hoyt Street subway to his cramped, damp, ludicrously expensive closet-sized apartment seemed somehow more threatening—darker, grimier, passers-by more foreboding. On one occasion he was mugged, barely thirty feet out of the mouth of the subway exit, coming back from drinks with the owner and a music promo director who wanted to get into features. Two guys: not the dark and grimey shadow men he'd been on the look-out for, but neat, clean-ish, one black, one white, with one knife between them, a hand clamped on his wrist and the blade, hidden from sight, pointed at the middle of his UniQlo button-down. He'd forked over the best part of two hundred dollars and his Samsung Galaxy, complete with the pictures of Sue that he was getting around to one day probably deleting.

New York began to simultaneously close in on him and slip away from him. He realised he'd made no connections outside the office (where people were professionally amicable and little more, barring the odd lip-loosening drinking session), that all his time in New York had involved working, being with Sue or being alone. He found that he was twenty-seven, and in the unexpected position of having to make friends, again, and not having the faintest idea how to do it. He tried the nascent internet dating systems—Craig's List,

FriendFinder—but found them disheartening, the women cold or disinterested or obviously psychotic, and he, he found, had no idea how to attract through text. He'd always thought himself charming, but now he was confronted with a different self he somehow could not escape: monosyllabic, literal, serious, try-hard. No matter what he tried, he could not escape this long chain of things not working out. His work relationships suffered. Suddenly, he found conversations trying. He had no quips—had to play-act at casual jocularity, and it came out needy, and he found the co-workers he'd been working up to calling friends no longer stopped by his desk, looked wary or uncomfortable when he stopped by theirs. He began frequenting a Korean bar off 33rd Street after work, drinking until closing, usually alone, staggering home. He was mugged two more times.

It was in this fug, eye-bagged and wan, bad-skinned and tired, contemplating what fate awaited him back in Seoul, when he met Eun Kyoung. In the Korean bar, alone, with a lunchtime beer and a kimchi-seafood pancake, he'd noticed her come in: this diminutive smiler wrapped in a coat and fur hat, clearly fresh from Seoul, speaking in Korean on her cellphone, wide-eyeing her surroundings. He tried to disguise his sly glances, eyeing her as she picked at a soybean jiggae, whilst the phone call, obviously with her mother, went on and on. No, she was saying, she'd tried everything but there was no way, she'd need to sort something else out— but surely that would take, what, a month? And where was she to stay until then? It seemed from what he could gather that she'd come to New York expecting to room with a family contact, but that the family contact's landlord had discovered the plan, declared it an illegal sublet, and threatened to have her evicted, leaving Eun Kyoung fresh from Seoul and with nowhere to go, and no-one in the city to help her. Excuse me, Kim Dae Woo said in Korean, once he'd heard the phone call finally draw to a close. I couldn't help hearing—

He turned to her, wiping his mouth, but as he did he saw his miscalculation. She was midway through dabbing tears away from her mascara'd eyes, and rabbit-in-headlights at his imposition. Oh, hey-- I'm sorry—

No, she sniffed, hurriedly tucking her tissue back into her purse, it's okay. I'm having kind of a bad day, and she laughed, wet eyes suddenly glistening, and Kim Dae Woo found he'd fallen, in that one instant of broken smile, or maybe, in retrospect, in the build up from her first entrance, vulnerable and flustered, to that climactic broken smile, perfectly in love with this diminutive smiler, fresh off a plane. As if his heart literally opened up at that point, from this dead, closed, knuckled thing, inflating back to full bloody life with a rush that made him so light-headed he thought he might fall off his stool. He found his ability to interact with another human magically returned—not only that, he was confident, brave, bold, calm. He joined her at her table, ordered them coffees, and shared the story of his first day and night in New York: how he'd lost the address of his pre-rented apartment, wandered aimlessly, jetlagged and disoriented, around the Lower West Side, certain he was going to be murdered, waiting for his parents to wake up, check their messages, and text the address through to him, until finally after close on seven hours dragging his luggage around he'd found his itinerary, complete with address, neatly tucked within the front pocket of his suitcase. She listened with such warmth, such unadulterated, doubt-free warmth that he felt that, tacitly, with no mention of it or even any overt flirtation, that they'd somehow agreed, already, to become a couple. You know, there's a guy in my office who's looking for a roommate. That's what I was going to say when I said hi.

Before you revealed your most embarrassing secrets you mean?

Oh—I've got way worse than that! The only thing was, he told her, the guy's a homosexual, so she'd have to be okay with that. Her smile faded for a moment as she thought about it. Oh... well, I guess it's New York, so... I guess it's okay? She made it a question, so he could have the final say on whether it was okay or not, which he agreed, since it was New York, it was, and he thought: yes, this is one you could have as a wife.

Four months later, his internship finished, they returned to Seoul, engaged, and Eun Kyoung pregnant. They rushed through a marriage, aware that if the baby were born a discreet five or six months post-marriage then judgemental relatives would make considerably less noise about conception not only outside Korea but out of wedlock too. The morning of their wedding day was a perfect storm: photo-shoots in the streets of Myeongdong, in the multi-storey wedding centre's photography suite, Eun Kyoung resplendent in an enormous, meringue-like gown, he with his hair fresh-trimmed and quiffed, three hundred friends, family and acquaintances gathered in the cavernous chapel, his father dour and proud swapping military service stories with Eun Kyoung's dad, their mothers watery eyed and gregarious, great aunts and uncles doddering happily, college pals, drinking buddies—it was all they could ask for, all that was expected of them, Eun Kyoung's small tummy pout hidden in the brilliance of her dress. And yet, as their retinue shuffled to the lunch room on the fourth floor for the post-wedding buffet, the previous wedding's guests still shuffling out in the opposite direction, and as he watched Eun Kyoung chattering beamingly with girlfriends, cousins, aunties, Kim Dae Woo found that all he could think about was Sue.

The storm has not passed, but lulled. The Danish director has sobered somewhat, leaning back in his seat straight-backed, staring blankly. The driver is yawning.

So you didn't know she was coming, huh? Your wife?

The director exhales deeply. No. We... we haven't been talking much.

Kim Dae Woo nods, checks his phone. Nothing from the noraebang queen. He realises he didn't give her his phone number.

Mm. Marriage, huh. It's a challenge. He sees the driver yawn again.

Is it? the director says.

Is it a challenge?

That's what you said, right? Still staring blankly, his voice a throaty murmur, Kim Dae Woo can't tell if the director is being antagonistic or just making conversation.

Well yeah—yours is perfect? Aware that came out testy, he smiles, forces a laugh. All plain sailing? C'mon.

The director looks at him. Your English is very good you know.

Ah yeah— *komapsumnida*, he intones in best supplicant voice, doffs his head in a mock reverent bow. It's the first time he's seen anything like a smile on the director's face since he picked him up from the airport.

No, he says, my marriage is not perfect. My wife... he rubs the bristles on his chin for several long moments. I don't know. It's complicated.

Well yeah, she's a woman! The laugh he draws from the director is minimal, and he worries for a moment that he might be one of these feminist men, that he must shift from locker room, boys-will-be-boys jocularity into sensitive modern-manism. This is a mode with which he is out of practice. No, I mean— it's always a challenge with men and women, right? That's just how it is.

Why? he murmurs. The car crosses a junction and takes a sideward storm wind shunt.

Because we're not the same. I have to be a man, she has to be a woman. Some women don't wanna be women, some wanna be men. And some men wanna be women. And either way no-one seems to know which is which anymore! Put that under one roof, throw in a couple of jobs and a kid— I call

104

that a challenge.

You love your wife? he says, and looks Kim Dae Woo in the eye.

Kim Dae Woo finds himself swallowing. Sure. She's my wife. You?

The Danish director looks away, nodding silently.

Arriving at their destination—an upmarket love motel in Haeundae in the area that passes, more or less, for a red light district—the car discovers the tail end of the typhoon. A street back from the beachfront the winds are manic, the rain fat and sidewards, so heavy the windscreen loses all visibility a second after the wipe of the wipers, leaving the driver, cursing under his breath, blind for a further second until the wipers repeat their action. Slowed to a fifteen-mile-an-hour crawl he turns into the motel's breakfront, guided by glowing neon signs refracting through the storm water, and shelter. They can hear the tumult barracking the city: gusting the rooves, flooding, howling in the darkness, whistling, screaming, like all the ghosts of the city's past have returned to vent their ghostly spleens on the solipsistic living of the city's present. The Danish director puts a clammy hand on Kim Dae Woo's knee. Thanks for everything, he says. Ask him to pick me up here tomorrow.

Okay, enjoy your four hours of sleep—you know we've got the panel discussion at noon?

He nods, pats his knee. Kim Dae Woo feels an unexpected bud of affection blooming in his gullet, and has the urge to hug the Dane. He swallows it. You'll be alright?

He downturns his lined mouth, opens his door. The ghosts' furore peaks. We'll see, he says, and with a fairly accurate *koh-map-soom-nee-da* for the driver, he exits.

Left in the car, Kim Dae Woo stares for a moment. It's two weeks since he saw his wife, and he did not make his promised evening call the previous evening. It is pushing 3am.

You think the storm's almost done? he asks the driver. The driver exhales an aspirated string of consonants. Yeah. Take me back to the noraebang.

\ *kittisak* \

MY NAME IS Kittisak. It is a common name, but you will not know it, like you will not know my face. Let me sketch myself for you: imagine the most beautiful frog you've ever seen. Can you see it? See the curve of its lip, how it rises back toward its luscious jowl, the thickness of its throat, the weedblack glimmering eyes? That's me. Nice to meet you.

I am a rising star of the independent scene. I know this because it says so in the festival brochure. *In Auspicious Malady, rising star of the independent scene Kittisak Charoensap dazzles as a disgraced police officer given one last chance for redemption by the last person he expects... his long lost daughter.* A subtle indie three-hander, the daughter shows up at my country house in the dead of night with a young man she says is her fiancee—but I know there's something off with him, and as night presses in, and rice whisky loosens tongues, revelatory truths are uncovered, and there appears a loaded gun. It's not half bad, for something so cheap.

And what leads you to so consistently seek out and work on ambitious, independent productions like this one? asks the beautiful panel host. Her glittering eyes are the colour of plums, her pant suit direct from Milan. Korea is particularly good at producing magnificent women. For a moment that elongates my mind travels back to a hotel room in Singapore in 1987, and Choi Sun Mi, naked backed, sitting up in bed, sheet to her breasts, gazing out over Marina Bay. I was still a tadpole, galavanting on father's dime. I remember stroking her back—I think—was that her? Didn't she say—yes--she said

Doesn't the water seem like time?

and I snorted a young idiot's snort—no--did I? No—I looked out—or am I rewriting?—over the bay, the flash and glimmer of the sun on the water—or am I doing that now, in my memory?—and said something like

How do you mean?

Maybe young me snorted and poked her, teased, maybe it's old me, now, saying to her, Sun Mi

Tell me what you see

and yes, that must be it, because there's no answer coming—just the angle of her cheek, her hair, dark as ginseng syrup, swept back, as she gazes out over the water of time, and the lines of her beautiful back—

What leads me to these kinds of projects? Well—my stool squeaks as I shift, the microphone swallows a shriek. They've left the lights up so I can see the crowd perfectly. A hundred or two eager eyes. Well, I'm not... how do you say... I'm not a spring chicken. The owners of the eyes laugh generously. I don't have a lot of time left, I tell them, for working on projects that don't interest me, or that don't try to do something, ah...

Artistic? offers the magnificent woman, and the feelings I'm re-experiencing for Sun Mi wash over her—even, yes, the image of Sun Mi, the image memories that I can access: there's a photo I remember, a smile, a creased nose—

Artistic, yes. I'm only interested these days in... in artistic value. Or, shall we say, principally interested. I still require a paycheque.

Another generous laugh, and a beam of approval from my new locus for Sun Mi. Choi Sun Mi... thirty-two years gone— she might for all I know (good God) be dead.

The panel becomes uninteresting quickly. The Dane with the holes in his ears is barely monosyllabic, and the Korean writer-director gives his answers in Korean, with no translation. My new Sun Mi handles them both with the utmost professionalism, never looking bored or robotic. And where did I meet Sun Mi, my real Sun Mi—ah! The Hyatt in Bangkok! A gala, or... some charity reception, chilled white wine and squares of quiche, tom yum vol-au-vons. I'd been dragged there by my father. Yes, yes, I remember—I'd been in the height of my youthful cockiness, full of repressed fury at my father, gleefully letting it show by sleeping with every woman in sight, and I'd seen her, in a strapless dress, sulking between the quiffs and combovers. Ah, those were the days... I had a hundred different ways of making the first move and didn't care who knew it. What did I say to her? Will the words come back to me? Was it something like...

Please tell me you're just here for the booze too? Or

Let me guess: toothpaste heiress? No, no... laxatives! Or

I'll give you a hundred thousand baht right now if you sneeze into that guy's Chablis.

Or something equally vacuous. But what does it matter? Who am I kidding—of course it matters. I'd give my weekends with the kids for a transcript of that evening.

You did a masterful job, I tell the new Sun Mi, once the crowds have dispersed, and she looks up from her cellphone, surprised, then smiling—genuine? Maybe.

Oh that's so nice of you to say, thank you. I have like a dozen of these this week, she says, with a cute eye roll.

Lucky crowds, I say, and hold my eyes on her until her mouth creases upwards. So, where's good to go in Busan? I say. She asks if I'm alone, and I confirm. If only I had a knowledgeable, beautiful local to take me out for the evening, I say.

Khun Kittisak, she says, in decent Thai, placing her fingertips on my forearm, you're the same age as my father!

But I'm not your father, I say.

Yesterday's typhoon has left its mark on the city: everywhere, fallen branches, broken awnings, rugs and slipmats hung out to dry over railings. She speaks in Korean to the taxi driver, and we slalom down a side street with a swash of flood water, past a shadowy bus depot and a row of open-fronted seafood and beef-bone stew shacks. She takes me to a hot pot joint, steamed up windows, families sitting on floor cushions around low tables, bubbling meaty concoctions. So, she asks, as she cuts a spool of rice noodles with giant red-handled scissors and lets them fall into our broth, are you enjoying the VIP experience? Her eyes are striking—they make sparkling strikes at my insides.

Oh, I see—this is a service you provide for every panel guest huh? *Agashi*, you wound me. I thought I was special to you.

I provoke another eye-roll, this one more coy than cute, a sideways head tilt. This, I see, is a nervous habit, overused. Subsconsciously performative. Khun Kittisak, not what I meant na? She adds the Thai 'na', correct intonation. I meant... she flaps out her arms as she looks for the right phrase—this too is performative. She elongates the pause with her lean arms outstretched, her chest pressed forwards, lets me sit in the silence, then... I meant the *festival experience*. Chai mai?

I give her my yes/no smile. It works not just on camera. If this evening is anything to go by, I tell her, my festival experience is rapidly improving. She head-back-laughs—I've played my part. Some people are looking for conversational dance partners, and she knows now she's found one. She opens her seated stance, edging her lap towards me, widening her shoulders, and I wonder how she might taste. So how long did you spend in Thailand?

She adjusts her feathered sweep of hair. Three years, off and on.

In Bangkok?

Chai ka. Our company has offices there. Actually, my husband is Thai.

I leave the silence for her to fill. We can both play the confidence game.

Ex-husband, she says, and for a moment her mask creases downwards with regret, or something like it. When I met Sun Mi, she'd been on the rebound too. Some Korean trust fund kid who'd promised her the world. She told me all about him, over... what was it... over

noodle soup

yes!

basil and celantro and five spice and steam

some hi-so joint by the Chao Phraya, river boats sloshing the water towards the pier. She told me all about him — can't remember the details, but

she'd cried

or almost

watery eyed

and I'd told her something like

You can let yourself cry over that jerk or you can let yourself learn a lesson.

and something stirred inside her, and she came back to the condo apartment my father was paying for in Sathorn, and we played cassettes on a wall-mounted hi-fi system and took each other's clothes off. And what did she taste like, Choi Sun Mi, when I buried my head between her legs? And I flew her to Singapore for that long weekend by Marina Bay, and she gave me her thoughts on time? Sun Mi-shi... what happened

112

to you my darling? Are you still on my side of the world? Are you in this same city even? Are you still here on Earth? Have you come back to me, in this different woman's body?

Come back to me, Sun Mi-shi

bring me one good memory...

I wake in our apartment (our apartment!). It's dark outside—middle of the night. The frosted windows let through a miasmic glow from the street lights, like as if a distant exploding star had been frozen in time. One of my earplugs (yes! I slept with ear plugs!) has fallen out. I pat around the bed but can't find it. That's when I realise: she's not there. God, I can feel the tiny dull stab in the sleep-confused heart. Sushi? I call out, dry-throated.

(Sushi! I used to call her Sushi!)

I can hear her violin.

The lights of the sitting room are blazing. We haven't washed up (the maid comes tomorrow) and there's a pot on the stove with the dregs of tom kha: forest dark lime leaves and lemongrass swirls. The music is coming from the balcony. I pad my dreamy feet over the floor tiles, the rug—thick and soft, on the floor in front of the TV—and look through the glass of the sliding doors. There she is. In her white nightgown, foot up on the balcony railing, sat on her stool, instrument pressed down into her shoulder by her jutted chin, and she's playing a minuet, muted by the glass, and I slide it open. You'll wake the neighbours, I say, and she smile-shrugs up at me. She is the most beautiful thing I have ever seen in my life. Small price to pay, she says. But I'll stop. And she does.

Peach?

Hey, I was gonna call you. Your son hit his head.

He what?

Yeah, we were—hey! Put it down! We were messing around and he hit his head on the side-table. There's a little cut. Should I take him to the hospital?

How little?

Hmm... little. And a lump.

Give him some candy and tell him he's fine. No, put him on.

Okay, hang on.

...Daddy?

What happened?

I hit my head.

Are you okay?

There's a lump and it hurts a little but not too much. It wasn't Peach's fault, he was just playing the throw-me game.

No more throw-me game.

...Mm.

Okay?

Okay. Are you coming back soon?

Glad you're okay little warrior, now put khun Peach back on.

...So what do I—

He's fine. Listen, Peach, something's come up. Can you

keep them another few hours?

I *knew* it! Who came up?

None of your business.

Some things never change huh? Okay, three hours, max, but then I have a drinks meeting with some Americans. I'm really, really not a babysitter man.

Three hours is perfect. Take them to the aquarium, they've been begging to go—I'll pay.

Three hours!

I promise, I'll meet you at the aquarium, okay? My libido thanks you.

I'm honoured.

Hey—put a band aid on his cut, okay? There's some in the bathroom. He likes the ones with superheroes on.

My hotel room is golden-hued, the bed a queen, and all overlaid with corners and colours of that room in Marina Bay, 1987. For a while at least. But it drifts. My new Sun Mi wipes her inner thighs with tissue. Her beauty was no mirage, it has not faded, physically, but something has. I wish we could smoke in here, she says, rolling her pretty head onto my chest. I smooth the treated carpet of her hair. Sun Mi smoked too—we all did back then. For a moment, I think I can taste her kiss on my lips, but it's just a similar recipe.

\ *delicacy* \

SHE REACHES

her twenty-fourth birthday with the glass around her organs mostly intact. There had been one or two incidents but who couldn't say the same? Once, on her year in Bremen, she'd gone dancing with a lugubriously handsome football player from the university B team and contracted some kind of fracture that had spiderwebbed around her pancreas. She'd felt it spreading inside: the cracking of the sugar on a toffee apple. Bruises bloomed on her abdomen, jellyfishing to the surface before your very eyes, midnight blue. He'd been nice—sat with her in the emergency room, brought her spritzkuchen to cheer her up, smiled a rumply smile under terrified-guilty brows. He wasn't a bad guy, in his way. Henrik was it? Henning?

By the time she moves into the flat in Islington with Lucy she's become a not insignificantly successful writer. For the online arms of broadsheet newspapers, mostly, and zeitgeisty American or American-esque zines. She is the Glass Organs Girl. Her piece for the New Yorker was something of a hit. Malcolm Gladwell had emailed: what a terribly interesting article, the email had said. What a terrible and interesting article. He went on to explain over several paragraphs that he didn't mean terrible in a pejorative sense, and to suggest that she let him know 'the next time you're in New York' so that she could come over and meet him and his wife, try his boeuf Bourgogne, and he could pick her brain—if that, too, wasn't encased. Ha ha.

Comporting oneself with grace becomes a habit. She learns to walk on invisible cushions of air. She wears a see-through raincoat around Shoreditch, as wry self-commentary slash self-promotion—there goes that Glass Organs Girl. Her brain, in fact, is not encased, and she relishes throwing her head backways and sidewards when laughing, flicking her feathered hair, relishes the bounce, the little headache, the worried looks she attracts. One of these days, Lucy said to her one night, after too many gin and tonic and cassises, all your insides are going to shatter, and all that stuff inside is just gonna... just gonna leak right out like diarrhoea. She tells Lucy that that was probably a bit fucking far, and puts her to bed, wiping the hair away from her sweaty forehead, and considering the normality, the primacy of Lucy's organs, pulsing and beating away in her body, hot and wet and drunk and suited to their environment. She thinks it really was a bit fucking much actually.

iv.

THERE ARE geese on the roof of the nationalmuseet. Real, no fooling geese.

Why do you sink they got up there? says the Writer, shifting the beagle-ear collar of his cardigan.

You mean how?

No, no— he wipes his stubble-encircled mouth.

The first kiss had been a drop-kick:

I'll punt at you from range...

The second closing in like a collapsing scrum:

I had a feeling about you...

Why are they up there? I dunno. Part of their territory? I pick at the space next to my mouth where I can feel the pressure of phantom silicon.

I sink their terrytory is only by water, no? He looks at me from behind his eyelashes, and beyond him a German family picture-pose. I want to fill his pockmarks with the liquid of my heart.

Well, how bright can geese be? I say, and smooth his sleeve.

He makes a face. I've let him down. Nature always has a reason, he says. A wing beats overhead, a Metrobus elongates around a traffic island. We walk towards the Strait of Øresund. There are flocks of afternooners on the islands by Nyholm, beering around tables, leg-dangling over the water. I am the spectre of myself.

And then again: the monster.

I'd fled the set still in my prosthetic. Fled? No, the panic had panicked itself out by then. I simply pulled up my jacket and balanced a hat. The set was in Nørrebro, near the University Hospital—I told the driver to head for nightlife. On we'd driven, through the rosemilk evening, him eyeing me in the rearview, myself peering back at me, what there was of me: the great hideous cursed clifftop of prosthetic and me. The rosemilk swirled through the buildings, streets full of coated shadows. The windows, largely tinted, drew few looks—a couple of armswingers peered as they road-crossed; maybe they saw an incomphrehensible silhouette. He dropped me at Studiestræde. The looks I received—it was like white corpuscles in a bloodsteam identifying a virus. I felt the Danish breeze on my hands, my socked ankles, but felt only weight and heat and perspiration on my cheeks, my brow, my neck, and the flag was fluttering on Christiansborg. I drank long-necked bottled beer in a dance-bar off Vestergade, crammed in with the young professionals. The texts started coming: make-up was still waiting. I hadn't left the set had I? Had I?

Monster? Spectre? I let the dance-bar plasma swirl me into a kidney-shaped dancefloor, and I beat the dog, I turned the screw, I monkied the monkey, I mashed my potatoes—this brunette student trio bunny-bumping at the hilt of my hips; I sprang a pole in my character's chinos—or were they my own? Did I bring them from Teddington, along with my heart full of memories? There exists grey matter in the heart, enough for a hidden trove of past... I sweated so much my head slipped an inch down my neck. I bellowed in Mikkelsens' faces. I collapsed onto the duvet of a Christianshavn chain hotel.

Phones have no memories, despite the lingo. Tap clear and a shitstorm simply disappears. They have no more memory than a piece of paper. I located his contact details under his name, plus WRITER.

We'd met first in a cafe near Angel, hydrangeas spilling out of distressed glassware all down the bookshelf-wallpapered walls, and he'd told me that he'd seen my work. The play, online—the, ah... I sink is Webster?

Duchess of Malfi, I'd said, and he'd nodded. Then the producer had taken over. Generous funding etcetera, Danish-German co-production.

And then there I was, on the duvet in a chain hotel in Christianshavn, encased in silicon. I texted him. Come and see me. Don't tell the others.

Monster? Spectre? Man? Boy? Hydrangeas spilled down the faux-bookshelfed walls, and he told me he'd seen my work. Not too disgusted I hope, I'd said, a hot cup of mulch-water halfway to my lips. He rumpled his rumply brow. His hairline, I noticed, was unusually definite, and lower on one side than the other. I sought... he shrugged down his mouth, bobbed his head, but before he could tell me the producer took over again, and I mulch-watered, wafered, and watched him, this Writer, in between the necessary replies.

He arrived at the hotel just after ten. I am here, the text had said—contractionless, quipless. I sent the room number. The room smelled of ironing boards. I remembered the stacks of ironing in our kitchen, my mother ploughing through and folding. The window showed a slender stripe of Torvegade. His knock was gentle. The door was unlocked, but I went to it, opened. The wetness of his eyes took me aback.

What happen? he said, shallow-breathed. I had so many questions, but I asked them only of the ether, and settled for inviting him in.

How many times have you done that?

That? With man?

Yes. Not many, I think.

No, not so many. In my country...

Mm.

The rosemilk had turned coal. There were revellers outside. A wall-mounted flatscreen on mute.

But I'm getting ahead of myself. I sat in the window alcove, as he looked at me, concerned. I worry, he said. They might--

What, sack me? Doubt it. They've shot most of the bloody thing already.

He stepped a step closer, sat on the bed. He didn't know what he was doing here.

So out we went, prosthetic and all. I asked him to show me somewhere the tourists don't know, and he led me to a small Lebanese pace behind the Tivoli. Paper tablecloths and babaghanoush. The waiter nearly shit himself. The Writer had a quiet word, and we were led to a dim table away from the windows. He ate olives and regarded the matter surrounding my head, began slowly to soften. I spilled wine down my chin. How is like? To be... you know, wiz zis?

To be out with it on? Um. It's... the same.

He raised one sheepherders eyebrow. A handsome couple were watching us from across their muhamara. How the same? he said.

I shrugged. No answer came to mind that could make it clear, and so we ate warm fluffy pitta and fists of grilled lamb, and I asked about Syria. You couldn't read beneath his mask, if a mask was what is was. He talked as if he was talking about a school he once went to, a house he once lived in— nothing more than that. Is gone now, mostly. The country I knew. Is still very bad there.

You will go back?

One day, yes, sure. I am still Syrian. I still have an uncle and a cousin, in Damascus.

I almost asked where the rest of his family was.

The first kiss, it was a punt, a hail Mary—

The second a collapse...

We wandered Vesterbro, and the streets were drunker now, gobbier, young bucks gobsmacking, yowling, running up to touch, and so I peeled off a flank of temple just to see them spit.

Come on, let's get this off you, he said, and took me back to the hotel.

He sat me on the en suite counter-top and peeled me. Strips coming off like goose flesh. I felt it tug and release my skin with a sting, saw myself pink-speckled in the rimlit mirror. I let him dab at me.

What did you think of my play?

He looked surprised. Remember? The Duchess of Malfi? Back when we met, in London—

Yes, yes, he said, looking at the strip of sticky flesh in his hand, things coming back to him. I sought you were beautiful.

The rosemilk had turned coal, blackbright. Revellers outside, flatscreen on mute.

How long has it been? That I've been 'missed'?

Hm. Like... five or six hours? Is midnight now, almost.

I rolled closer to him, head newly nude. He had bruises on the hilt of his hip. Gooseberry blue.

How many hours shall we ask for? From the hour gods.

He smiled.

There are geese on the roof of the nationalmuseet.

Why do you sink they got up there?

THE FIRST TIME

I ever made love with anyone was during Wayne's World 2. It all happened during that bit with Rip Taylor and Waynestock, before the Graduate parody. Earlier, there's a sequence in which Garth loses his virginity with Kim Basinger. Nervous, his bottom lip shaking, she tells him

Take me, Garth

and he says

Where? I'm low on gas and you need a jacket.

But then she pounces, and afterwards he becomes Garth Hephner, in smoking jacket, puffing on a bubble pipe. We were on the sofa in her bedroom—a giant room with an L-shaped layout, double bed in one corner, drumkit next to it, sofa on the other side (the low-slung, saved-from-the-skip type) and a portable TV sitting on an entertainment station above an N64 with three controllers.

We'd been together something like two months, bandmates for six. She'd wanted us to be called The Disabled, on account of her hearing. But *we're* not disabled, Charlieboy had said, thwacking at his unplugged bass. Come over here, she'd said, brandishing a drumstick, I can sort that out. D'you want it in your ear or up your arse? At school she'd elevated herself:

victim in year seven, eight, she seemed to have decided somewhere along the line that she didn't give a fuck. By year ten she was guesting for local bands in venues across town, taking the kit for Agnostic Cavalcade, The Anti-Me, and her uniform became less and less standard: trou, elbow-length sleeves, blue fringe, tattoos (a Wu Tang W on her wrist, a Nirvana lithium smiley behind an ear lobe). She'd play up her hearing aid instead of hiding it, shout-talking back to douchebags: What? You'd like to do *what* all over my tits? Her fearlessness wasn't performed either—that would've been see-through. It was real. God knows how she did that. Maybe it was always in her, but it made her a local celebrity. Lads who thought Embrace were alternative would show up to her gigs with fake IDs, neck Carling and fumble their juvenile post-gig flirtations, get chucked out. Older guys too—local scenesters, ex-junkies, hard punkers, pushing forty, would drape themselves over her in smoking areas, share rollies, pretending to be avuncular. She knew what they wanted, and they didn't frighten her either. Do you wanna write my sixteenth birthday down in your diary? I'd heard her ask one of them, before he snuck off back to the bar, flush-cheeked and beaten, by this five-foot-nothing drummer girl with the hearing aid and the blue fringe.

So we were on the skipbait sofa in her jam-room-slash-bedroom, and Garth was becoming a man. We were curled up together, interlocked, post-jam, just the two of us, had been going through out retinue, dicking around with bad Zeppelin covers, Deftones, and her neck, slightly sweat slicked, was giving off that scent: shampoo and fresh bread. She's pretty hot huh, she said. She's like the go-to hot chick for this era eh.

Who?

Basinger, and she shifted around, repositioned a leg.

Yeah I guess so. What was she in?

Dunno. Loads of eighties stuff I think.

Right. Outside you could hear her neighbour cutting the grass, calling to his wife. We kissed, undressed, as we tended to do. She said her parents would be out until later. Wayne was engaged in a kung fu showdown with Cassandra's father. The four months we'd been bandmates before becoming more had started unremarkably. She'd had the band going a year already, but her friend dropped out, 'artistic differences', and Charlieboy recommended me, so in I came, with my cherry red SG Ibanez and wobbly power chords. She answered the door, that first jam, in skater jeans and a blue strappy top over a white strappy top, the lines of her arms and shoulders on show, and a little hole opened up in my stomach—just a coin-sized hole, nothing earth-shattering, but it made me want to smell her. I stood near her so I could, in the kitchen, leaning against the counter, the three of us sinking stubbies of generic French lager that she produced from a room off the garage, and her scent, when I'd catch it, produced a waterfall of endorphins somewhere around the base of my skull, down my neck. She had whisps of cat-brown hair spooling loose from her scrunchie, from behind her hearing aid, this slender soft body. We jammed My Own Summer, The Sweater Song, me and Charlieboy alternating ropey vocals, improvised some dumb-dumb drop-D pound-alongs, feedback skrawks. I did my comedy Slash, my Angus Young, and I saw her beaming, laughing, thrashing out silly faux-Bonham fills, knocking over her own hi-hat, creasing up. The three of us slouched in the living room with more stubbies after, laughing and glowing and feeling like we could eat the world, in front of back-to-back episodes of Futurama. In one, the Robot Devil tricks Leela into marrying him. It's too bad, because Fry has learned how to love. He loves the one-eyed Leela, the ass-kicking, ship-piloting Leela, because, underneath, they're the same. The Robot Devil is smarter than Fry (everyone is), but Fry is sincere, like a child. He wears his heart on his sleeve. And a sincere heart on a childlike sleeve is worth a lot, it turns out.

So we undressed, as we tended to do, and her body was beautiful in a way that can't be described, in the way that water is beautiful in the desert maybe, or how air is beautiful when you come out of a sauna. If we're gonna bone, she said, we should pause Wayne's World, with her usual unshakeable, unflappable humour. No—*leave it on*, I said, in romance-voice, and she laughed her big good laugh. I'd had sex before, twice, with the same girl: drunk in her house at the end of a house party, and again, a fortnight later, at the end of another house party. We'd hid the blood-marked sheets in a cupboard the first time. The second, I was too drunk to remember.

In the movie, Wayne's paranoia alienates Cassandra, foists her into the arms of Christopher Walken. Cassandra had been growing famous, destined for big things, and Wayne was still just Wayne: goofy bad-haired joker-boy with an Aerosmith fixation. He has to see the error of his ways, come close to losing everything, before he can have a chance at winning her back, via a Charlton Heston cameo and a race to the church. The four months before coupledom, she'd started taking over my waking thoughts, my dream life too, this fearless girl whose smell turned me to jelly. But not just fearless, no— kind. Gentle. She'd check that others were okay before doing anything for herself. She'd offer round her chips, her crisps, she'd find a spare chair for anyone joining your group, give up her own. I noticed she laughed at my jokes, even the not- really-jokes, the semi-quips. She started giving me lifts, in the silver Nissan Micra gifted to her by her over-generous Dad. There was a hug, a kiss, a hand-hold, texting. Texting was still new then—just black block letters on a little green screen. She said, I can read lips you know, and I tested her out. That's gibberish, she said, correctly. Okay, okay, and I tried it out for real. She nailed every word. I asked her what it was like without the hearing aid. Well I've always had it, so... some people say it's like being underwater. I stuffed foam earplugs in my ears, the kind guitarists use to stop tinnitus, until she told me to cut it out. Years later, I would actually develop tinnitus, after a couple years of touring with The Band Who Shall Remain Nameless. This roiling backgound sea that creeps up on you until one day you realise it's got you, and there's no way of going back.

So we undressed, as we tended to, and tended to each other, and all of a sudden we were doing it, on the skip-bait sofa, as Wayne raced to the church, and I found the unshakeable humour had gone out of her eyes—her shields were down. You don't need the details. I told her afterwards I loved her, the first time I'd said that, and she whinnied with happiness and curled up into my lap, said it back. We rewound the movie—on video, folks—so we could rewatch the ending, and let ourselves enjoy the remaining feeling of presence, solitude, togetherness, that feeling of infinite warmth you get curled up with a lover as twilight settles, before her parents were due back.

Years later, deep in the throes of tinnitus, at my wits end from this constant thrum, I'd find myself frequenting the same pub as Ralph Brown. Ralph Brown, aka Danny the Drug Dealer from Withnail & I, aka Del Preston from Wayne's World 2. I'd see him at the open mic nights, hosted by his nephew, watch him play a Take That cover on the communal keyboard to twenty-odd receptive week night drinkers. I'd work up the courage to perform myself, stage nerves and anxiety having gripped me in the most profound way after the collapse of The Band Who Shall Remain Nameless. I'd play songs I'd played for her, way back when, in her room, just the two of us, dicking about: Be Quiet And Drive (Far Away), Good Riddance, Where Did You Sleep Last Night. I'd get to know Ralph, shout him the odd Guinness, get a Doom Bar in return, and I'd tell him one night about Alice with the hearing aid, Alice of the lip readers, how we'd done it with his movie in the background, and he laughed, slapped his thigh. I'd tell him how I'd broken her heart. I didn't tell him that I still dreamt of her, fifteen years later, that I'd sometimes imagine bumping into her, that I'd thought I had seen her once, through a crowd, in London, years ago, with the hurtful ex-partner who'd come to be known as The Ex-Fiance Who Shall Remain Nameless next to me, holding my hand. Thought I'd seen her see me, through the crowd, eyes widening, stop for a moment, as if she was thinking of pushing through to me, before the crowd took her away once more. He helped me with the tinnitus, Ralph did—his friend had it bad, knew ways to manage it. And you can—you can manage it. It never goes away, but you can manage it.

\ *star creature 2: genesis* \

IF I TELL you something, do you promise you can keep a secret?

Promise? On your mother?

What kind of person doesn't have a mother? Fine, your father then. Promise on him. You do? You swear it? Lips-locked and all that? Hearts crossed? I've gone with plural just in case you have two. Octopuses have three. You're not an octopus are you? No octopuses is fine darling, it's an acceptable variant. Don't come the syntactical pedant with me, you won't get very far.

So we're agreed? Promise been promised?

Alright then. Brace yourself.

I have the key.

No, not that kind of key. If you're going to be childish you can forget it.

What key? Well I'll tell you, if you'll listen. If you think you have the right kind of ears. Let me inspect them. Hm. Slightly hairy, but maybe they'll do. I suppose we could give it a whirl and see how far we get. Would you like that? Course you would. Gin and tonic thanks, triple. Well then a double and single and a nice little swizzler, good lad.

Thanks. What? Oh yes, the key. Well lean in then, do I

have to tell you to do everything? Are you ready?

I have the key to eternity.

What is it, you ask? The key to eternity? Well, I can't just tell you can I, that would hardly be fair. Think of all the poor buggers who've toiled their lives away, who've spewed up their guts in the search—and you expect to simply be told? Ask and ye shall receive? Pull the other one sunshine, it's got mandalas on. Have you ever wondered about Eastern religion? The detachment from all earth's treasures, love, family, *passion*—and all that illusion of the self stuff. Codswallop if you ask me. Let me riddle you this, Sonny Jim—if the key to peace means eliminating joy, is peace all it's cracked up to be? I mean, ultimately, you have to ask yourself if the monks are just playing with syntax.

Monks, sweetheart, monks. Try to keep up, if you haven't got the mental capacity for a fractured narrative—what's the *point* in A to B anyway? Is that how life is? In your experience?

What *is* your experience? No tell me, I want to know. I'm genuinely curious. Truly.

Really?

Gosh. For how long?

My. That is a long time. And you—?

No. I never would've guessed you know.

Speaking of long times, have I told you how I was formed? Formed darling, formed, it's like being born but more spectacular. I was formed in a white giant, deep within the star matter. How? Don't be tedious. You should be asking *why*.

136

Why? Well I could tell you of course, but you don't think it'd be more fun to figure it out yourself? Being spoon-fed is rarely as good as it sounds, depending on the context.

Suffice to say, somewhere in that nuclear sea of unimaginable heat, brilliantine heat, and light, matter-destroying world-eating light, and heat, I formed, and now I'm here, as you can see, and I have with me the secrets. Yes, plural. A cephalopod's circulatory system of secrets in me there is, and guess what my little dovelet, my little bird, my pretty little tubby-tummied piggy... wait, this place. It's all wrong. How far to yours?

Much better.

Yup, I'll share. I'm a sharer don'cha know. Turn that lamp on. And the big light off. Here, throw this over it. There. Much better. Mood matters, honey-buns. Anyone tells you otherwise, slap 'em and run, you're dealing with a nincompoop.

It *is* a good word, you're quite right, that's why I chose it. You might not be quite as thick as you look you know. Hm. Which makes you potentially... okay, better conduct a test. Look at this finger. No this one. That's it. Now look at the ceiling... and the wall... and the ceiling... and the other wall...

...'s that sweetheart? No, you had to sleep for a bit, don't you remember? There, keep your head down my love, no need to move around, you'll just make yourself woozy. There, take it easy. Ooh, you're burning up. Here, take a sip. Just water, more or less. Like you. Like all of you, your lot. Just water and sadness, aren't you, walking around, in your cities. Squishy bipedal sadness sacs, that's what I see when I see you. When you're being hurtful—sadness. Abusive—sadness. Cocky, noisy, howl-at-the-moon—sadness. You try to hide it, which is ridiculous in the first place—as if you could. I see with the light of a thousand moons, I see with all the shimmer on a galaxy of starlit seas, and do you know what I see?

Hm? Your scalp? Don't worry, I'll put it back on. Doesn't hurt does it? Well *tingles*, yes, no-one promised there wouldn't be tingling, what've you got against tingling? Haven't you ever tried an opioid?

Liar, what about that party in your second year, hm? No of course it wasn't just hash, you—never mind, this is a digression. Stop leading me down the garden path, naughty sausage.

What's that?

The key?

Oh.

Yes.

Yes I suppose I did didn't I. Here, one more sip.

That last little bit too.

Good lad.

So. You want to know about the key?

Well, probably shouldn't have taken that last little sip then should you. You know you're far too trusting. Still, who knows what kind of answers await you on the other side. No, strike that, it's nowhere near that binary. Sides! Ha. Well. I'm rambling aren't I. It's the gin.

One last what?

One last kiss?

From me?

What, you don't think I really liked you do you?

Oh, chicken.

Well. Go on then.

There.

Not so bad I suppose.

And then again... to be loved... I do hear you lot banging on about it. Incessantly... would you like another? One more before you go?

...Yes. There we are. Yes, there is something to it isn't there. Maybe it's because you're so close to...

Alright. I'm feeling...

Come here chicken. Lend me your ear. I did promise, sort of, after all. Come'ere and I'll tell you one of the secrets. Just to ease you on your way. Something to carry you out on a high.

You hear that rushing, on the fringe of your soundscape?

You hear it? Just staring to get louder?

Like water?

You know what that is? Can you guess?

Here: let me tell you...

You won't believe it when you hear it, it'll seem so obvious, but... well, that's always the way...

Shhh love, or you won't hear...

SHE IS STILL at school when she is cast as the

star of To Our Loves. Co-written by the bear-ish director, the film concerns a fifteen-year-old girl and her first experiences with promiscuity. Moving from lover to lover, the girl admits she is looking to fill the hole left by her father, who is played by the bear-ish director himself, appearing most prominently in a scene in which he slaps her realistically in the face. In the bedroom scenes she is photographed post-coitus, not mid-, and romantically—promiscuity is not presented as sin here, and her youthful nudity, like that of Psyche, Andromeda, is timeless, to be appreciated. She is the same age as her character. The French Academy gives her a Most Promising award.

\ *girth* \

IN ORDER TO ^{get big,}

get big, you need routine. Mornings four-to-seven are for toploading — sweat it out pre-dawn motherfucker! Jared's got this *dope* dope channel, Jimmie's saying, he's got it all man, *tell*ing you. Million subscribers, sells sups, cree, prote, he gets new videos on every *day*, he's real good on dynamic tension, weights-free — dude, are you on the weights-free tip yet? Weights-free is the *shit* dude, no I'm *tell*ing you, for real, you won't believe how huge you can get. Check me out man, check me out, right there, the delts — you see that? See that? That's weights-free dude, for real. Tried *ev*erything for that area, weights-free *tar*geted the *shit* out of it. The Stuntman stands in the light from the blinds three hours into a Highland Park morning, the scent of jacaranda through the cracked windows and Mikaël's cigarettes. He flies his arms up and back and down, up and back and down. He tenses his core. He pictures his core a barrel, and the core of the barrel a coal. Wouldn't it set the barrel on fire? Maybe if it was lit.

Keep *down* man!

Mikaël is frowning in the doorway to his bedroom. He had been rocking Wheatus.

Sorry man. He jabs his cellphone's volume tab.

Mikaël yawnfoots to the refrigerator, and stands in its coolness as he glugs from a carton of cree. Mikaël is huge. Like a bear on hind legs, standing by the refrigerator, glugging cree. Mikaël gets solid work tossing midgets out of rings. Mikaël is all girth. I mean check out Mikaël dude, Jimmie says, in his Honda Civic, on the way to the audition, you see the lugs on that guy? He's a *beast* man, you think motherfucker was born that way? I don't know how they breed 'em in St Petersburg but don't nobody breed motherfucken colossuses like *that* motherfucker. The traffic worsens. The Stuntman checks the time on his cellphone. It doesn't register—his mind was elsewhere—so he has to check again. We're gonna miss it man. The cars seem endless. Fuck, Jimmie says, jabbing the digital radio.

She has diamonds on the soles of her shoes

Yeeeeah, gon be tight brother, gon be tight as a nun's pucker. Ha! Nun's pucker! Even I don't know where that came from man, but I like it. Tight as a nun's pucker man. And Jimmie puck-puck-pops his lips.

Diamonds on the soles of her shoes

He is not big enough for the part. It's just one line, but they need it impactful, and that means huge. Your agent sent you down here for nothing, the casting assistant with the shiny forehead says. Seriously, whad're you, five-ten? One-eighty? You honestly think you're *big* big? Cause you're not. I honestly don't even know what you're doing here. I mean look around you—honestly. Do you know what you're doing here? Because I do not. He looks around. The other men look back.

Mornings three-to-six are chest and shoulders on Mondays and Thursdays, legs and core on Tuesdays and Fridays, sprints and shuttles in the park down by the empty river on weekends, hangover or no. Keep *down*! Mikaël says. He'd been rocking Buck 65. Oh, shit, sorry—sorry Mikaël. Mikaël bears in the refrigerator cool, one enormous beef-slab arm crooked on the top of the open door, eating falafel from the pack, glugging cree from the carton. His shorts—white mesh Clippers training shorts fringed with red trim—are held up as much by the outward bulge of his enormous thighs as by the waistband. He is, every part of him, bulk. Mikaël? The bear-man turns only his eyes, cree running down his giant's chin.

You push, he says, handing him the harness. It tries to pull him over as soon as Mikaël lets go—he has to tense his whole body just to stay in place, and stop from hurtling back towards the machine. Isn't this too much? Mikaël shrugs enormously as he falls into a moon-sized beanbag. If you are weak. He doesn't want Mikaël to think he is weak. He grips the harness firmly in both hands. The resistance is planetary, but he pushes, as instructed. How long you been here man? he asks later, as Mikaël rubs linament from a pot covered in pharmaceutical Russian stickers into his aching shoulders. Mikaël puffs out his bottom lip, says simply: Long. His hands are not hard, they are soft, ridged in a few spots by calluses from barbell friction. Like, since you were—what—how old *are* you? He makes a Russian facial expression which the Stuntman cannot decipher. I am what I am here, Mikaël says. I come… he wipes a greased hand over his nose. The linament has medicated the air. I come… I don't know. I was not Mikaël then. I was another somebody. His giant hands find the sore ridge of the Stuntman's muscle. I don't remember.

He checks the time on his cellphone. It doesn't register, so he has to check it again. Dude we're good man, we're good—we got, like, forty minutes, right? Chill. Here, toss the cree. He makes it just in time. The room is bright, and cool from the air con. The other men look at him, nod hi, turn back to their sides, their cellphones. This one's… fuck, like, six lines? Uh-huh. Niiice dude. Alright, you got this badass, you got this. Fuck it right in its ass motherfucker.

He finds the words come easily. The actress—she is a stand-in for the real actress, and older than the part, and wooden, as if she's been pulled from the office last minute—looks at him, in her nervous wooden way, just like someone else did once upon a time. She becomes her… once upon a time, their hearts shared a chest… once upon a time…

You'll work for scale, right? Sure. The older casting director is still looking at him, speaking softly with the producer, who is nodding and looking at him also. Alright. Well. Who're you with, Aiden? Polly? Polly. Well we'll send the contract over today, and, we'll… yeah we'll get you onboard. Sound good? Sounds great. Okay. Oh, hey, don't take this the wrong way, but, couldn't hurt to nudge the mass up a touch, this character's gotta be huge, right? We'll put you in touch with our nutrition guy, you'll love him. Whad're you taking sup-wise—cree? XX?

He sees Mikaël padding from his bedroom to the kitchen, but this time it seems different—it seems he's walking in his sleep. His eyes are slitted open and angled down, and his lower lip is drooping. He watches him—you're not meant to wake a sleepwalker. He sways a little, standing there, in the kitchen, barrelled and swathed, great warrior's buttocks in boxer briefs, calves like hams, like brisket. He seems to sniff the air. Exhaust, jacaranda, cigarettes. The Stuntman rubs his eyes, and redyellow pools flash over his vision, flash over Mikaël, if Mikaël is really there at all, or in transition, between two different Mikaëls. Either way—some giant man swaying ever so slightly.

\ *for sale* \

empty head

...my childhood was empty, I tell him, but I know how to fill myself up. I take a long drink from his fountain. He presses play. *What happens when you lose everything? Well you just start again. You start all over again.* He guides himself into me.

In my memories, there is always someone watching over me: a guide, protector, shepherd, watcher. I understand that these are fabrications.

basket case

...is she okay with girl-girl?

Ask her yourself, she's right here. I nod nod nod, find the cat's got my tongue. No biggie: they like 'em shy. Makes for a better story.

His t-shirt is Dookie: the whole album cover. That's old, I say. So's the asshole wearing it, he says, and chuckle chuckle chuckles. His tan is burned in. I ask about the rate. The usual, he says, with a wave of a mahogany hand. I'll sort it out with your fella.

clusterfuck

...if you look at the lights you can lose yourself, but the thing is you don't want to lose yourself, because if you lose yourself you become vacant of face or limp of body. One time, so it must be possible, I lost myself and remained vigorous, rapacious, so it must be possible, but it's much more likely you'll limp out and have to do the scene again, and the actor will be pissed and you can kiss the next six jobs that you were going to be recommended for goodbye. So the best way is, go the other way: yum it up like it's salad, just gorge yourself, give em what for, don't overthink, just play the part, be the vixen. There are four this scene, four plus me, and three seem okay, the girl's kind of hot, though nasal and nose-jobby, but the fourth—stone cold narcissist, sociopath, heebie jeebies, but even for cats like him you can't check out totally, gotta lap him up, go to town, be the queen, spank the rump, rub the calf, glance at the light, let it blur, leave burn, yellow red, retina flash, clusterfuck, four plus you plus six crew plus whatever gods you think might be looking down, if you believe in that kind of up-above-us-looking-down, angel-on-my-shoulder mumbo jumbo...

five dreams

...the first: there are three of me. I run into the open square, but can't catch up to the other two. Buckets of toilet water slopping down from third floor windows.

The second: I'm back in my father's basement. Dani, he's calling out, Dani! But he's distant, and the boy is crawling around between my legs like some kind of cat, and the windows and doors are barred, but it feels good so all is okay, all is okay, and father's voice remains distant, Dani—

The third is a fuck dream: sticky icky in some asshole's car, and serial killers beyond the windows.

In the fourth, I'm with Mr Dookie. They tell me you were worth every penny, he says, and a mahogany hand strokes the sweat-slick hair from my brow. I don't doubt it, he says, with half a laugh in his sunshiney voice. We divorce, eventually, and he takes the kids, but they wanted to go with him. We just don't trust you mommy, they chorus, and he shrugs good-naturedly.

The fifth: floating above a roomful of naked corpses, balloon-like, bumping the ceiling, then it's a field, a park, the ocean, falling, sploosh, kick damn legs KICK

economics

...they're saying they'll pay top dollar.

Why? I barely knew her.

Bull, you were close, you said—sleepovers and shit? You just don't wanna do it, and, hey, no, I get that, but serious? There's no reason not to— I mean what kind of bargain is— when you're friends, it's not like— listen, I know you got like, you've told me there were, what, pills? Vicodin? You've got stories, so.

Yeah but. But I haven't seen her in, what, three fucking years. I don't know who she is *now*.

blurs

...I used to run home after work—change in the stock room into shorts and vest and run run run all the way, stop to squat, stretch, run run run, and the neighbourhood would become a blur, the spaces between the reference points stretching out like a 70s sci fi effect, between work, In & Out Burger, school, home, Kristen's place, Lee's place, all blurring into non-space, soup, and I'd circle the block for extra distance, shower in the little bathroom by the garage, pinch pinch pinch my thighs and ass and cheeks to see them pink, slap my face...

babies

...you know what? Mr Dookie's saying. The best mommas I know come from this business. Seriously. The absolute best. Kind, nurturing... know why? I tell him that I do not know why. I mean, I can't say for sure, but... well, a lotta our girls, they don't come from such good homes. So, I think it's that they know what it's like, you know? To *not* feel, you know... loved, or understood, or... you know? I nod that I do know. He takes off his sunglasses to scratch the skin beside his eye, and his eyes are bordered by a pale anti-shadow of lesser tan.

do you have the time

...to listen to me whine? About nothing and everything that I want? I am one of those melodramatic fools, neurotic to the bone no doubt about it. What is this? he says. Green Day, Dookie. Jason had it on his T-shirt, remember? Well whoopee for Jason. *Sometimes I give myself the creeps, sometimes my mind plays tricks on me, it all keeps adding up, I think I'm cracking up,* I like it, I say. These old bands are always singing about like neuroses and paranoia and... yeah, and all that kind of stuff. Guess it was a

big thing back then. You can fuck him, I don't mind, he says, just make sure you get some work out of it.

for sale

...So what can you give me?

Well— I mean, I don't know. It was a long time ago I knew her.

Two three years, not that long. Plus they were friends from, what, fourth grade?

From acting class.

But you're not close anymore?

No. We didn't fall out or anything.

So what can you give me? Drugs? Boys? Booze? Family shit? Don't be shy now, let me have it all.

I mean, we went through a vicodin phase.

Ha ha, course you did sweetie. How old?

Like fourteen. Not all the time or anything.

Was she a virgin back then?

I mean, so what? We were teenagers, you know? We had fun. My little brother, he lost his virginity when he was twelve, with my friend Sylvia. He was okay. He liked it.

How about Kristen? Was she twelve too?

No, I don't-- fourteen maybe. Me too. So?

empty stomach

...I've had an empty stomach all day, I tell him. So eat something, genius. No, I don't want to. So what are you telling me? You're baffling sometimes, you know that? We drive around, lie around, he takes us to the observatory. I love it up here: all the people, the view. You know how many movies have shot up here? Tons. Rebel Without A Cause for one. I'm'a be one of them, one day, you know? My vision up on a big screen. People talking about it, analysing it, reviewing it. C'mere baby. You know you're my baby, right? You have any idea how sexy you are? Someone's dog is ruffling through the cacti, snaffling the dried out twigs littering the side of the path. His eyes: between his squinted lids, grey-green.

two dreams

...the first: we're kids again, in her room, cuddling, nestled together, watching the kiss scene from Cruel Intentions, Sarah Michelle Gellar. Wanna try it? A smushing together, but something happens mid-giggle and it becomes tender. We keep right on cuddling. She tells me about Juanito, about pools of love. It happened just like this. She tells me about her dad, about her plans to leave as soon as she and her mom have enough money and can agree a plan. It's strangely peaceful, to be back in this moment. The window lets in shadows of jellyfish, clown fish, passing by.

The second: floating above a room of nudes, balloon-like, as they turn their eyes up to me, and the balloon begins to sink...

when I come around

...his body is hefty—pushing me down into his desk, something like a pen set digging into my back. Sorry sweetie, you wanna move to the sofa? Okay. He holds my hand as he walks me round, both of us waist-down nude. You're a natural, you know that? Not many are but you are. Gifted. Thank you Jason. You're gonna work, I mean consistent, don't worry about that. Thank you Jason. He kisses the top of my head.

IT'S THE TAIL ^{e n d} of the

first ACT and the band of heroes are fleeing the compound. Pyew, whizz, go the projectiles, and someone yells in cartoon terror. But look — the hand-operated cart is right there! Quick, flip the lever to shunt the tracks or we'll all be smushed by the crusher! Thank God, quick thinking, quip #14, flirt, straighten clothing, wink, quip #15, transition.

It's into the second act and the pace is lagging. A villainous figure appears in the shadows, tailing our guys in a purple Impala. You think you can lose im? Step on it, Joe! The camera swirls and whirligigs under the el train tracks, like The French Connection, but not. He tugs his charcoal grey lapels and makes an anachronistic comment. The colour grade is somewhere in the blue-orange realm.

There's a lovelorn character drama with a virile young beau who may be the big bad wolf. Chase me, chase me, through the pussywillows, through the Old Man's Beard, through the river. The men with guns are chasing too, and suddenly they're a team. They collapse panting, tractor-beaming each other's eyes. They don't yet know about the letter, but oh Lordy when they do…

Seven hundred superheroes kapow and bounce and ping-pong around seven hundred urban/space-station/jungle temple environment scenes. Representations of skyscrapers and transport pods and monoliths suffer significant damage. Your nephew pyews and kapows along in his seat, his eyes glowing in the light from the enormoscreen. No-one was hurt in the making, it says, but they always say something like that.

There's an art film, a disabled lead, trans issues explored, mellifluous subtext. The repressed actuary runs and runs through the cobbled streets, chasing the mysterious man-woman. The image shakes and shakes. He dreamed this chase in slow motion during the title sequence. When he catches the man-woman something as yet ill-defined will be revealed, and it will shake this city to its core, it will initiate the floods, and the third act will involve gondolas and revelatory confessions. You've seen his face before—early Almodovar, or that Argentinian thing.

There are tug-boats, hovercraft, rocketbikes, rollerboots. Over-shoulder come-on jibes, laser gun fly-bys, jawsnapping hounds that join mid-flight. Conveyor belt disaster aversions, weightless CGI swashbuckling. In one, the hero wakes up mid-chase and doesn't know what's going on. Oh, I'm chasing that guy, he realises, as he sees a miscrient running. Nope, he thinks, as the miscrient turns his way and fires, he's chasing me. The narrative jumps back, and shows us how he got here, and only then do we really understand.

V.

THINGS HAD ^{gone} _{well}

for the Teenage Actress, initially, then the knives came out. There was that dumb interview on TMZ.com, for one, with the person she'd thought was a friend, and then the issues with the dexedrine, which should never have been reported. One night she ran down a canyon naked, one piece said. But she'd not been naked—there was underwear, and six friends, and isn't that what nineteen-year-olds do?

She meets the Stuntman again at a party in the Hills, at her manager's boss's house. Hey—hi, she says to him. I haven't seen you in like forever. Since that crazy-ass thriller. He agrees that this is true, and seems intrinsically different. There's been a haircut, for one, and a shave, and his skin is glistening from some exotic moisturiser. He's bulked up too—she tells him so. Well, I'm going for character parts, he says. They told me I'm not a leading man, so, y'know, I need a niche. I've gone for Thug With A Heart of Gold. He's added a tattoo, she notices, and traces it with her finger. What does it mean? The answer he gives doesn't seem to explain, but answers so rarely do.

He tells her that with the help she gave him he was finally able to master the yank. It barely spooked him at all now, when the wire tautened, and off he took. His impact throes were amongst the best in the business, he'd been told by Steven Soderbergh's AD. I mean all that's behind me now though, pretty much, he says. My manager's rejecting all non-speaking parts. She grabs him and pulls his face into hers, in the glow of a streetlight off the Venice beachfront. I'm having a breakdown, she tells him, next to the pier, and the sea lions honk. He is understanding, as she knew he would be. She drives them to a taqueria. I feel like I'm melting, *all* the *time*. I feel like everyone's a fucking *robot*. I feel like we're bobbing around in a giant fucking fishtank. The counter guy is speaking Spanish to an older customer, and the bottles of beer are cold in the palm. He is listening in a way that seems attentive, so she goes on and on and on. I feel like I've murdered myself, she says. Like every good part of me has been thrown away. Like I'm made out of, fucking, fucking... tissue.

Used? he asks. She bursts out laughing. One word jokes can be the best.

They hold hands, for a while, down near the pier, walk in the oceanic breeze. It's good. Yes, it is. It's good.

IT'S HIM and some other guy it turns out—a knick-scalped ex-convict called Feliks. Alexei had told him it would only be him. So what? Alexei says, in the lay-by off the slip road to the airport, between sharp little sucks on his Pall Mall. What, you can't play nice?

Denis, the director, is sitting in the passenger seat of the six-year-old Lexus, staring blankly forwards. The passing traffic makes a sound like innards as it disturbs the ash-coloured slush. He has barely said a word since they picked him up. When Alexei had proffered the job, he'd made it sound different, and now he's looking at him, awaiting a response. Mikaël shrugs.

What's that supposed to mean? Alexei says, and eyes him for hard moment, before tutting, screwing his cigarette into the asphalt with his boot toe. Feliks, marble-headed from the cold, appears from over the roadside embankment, zipping up.

The snow has caused a string of cancellations, and the check-in area is chaos. Packs of angry Muscovites yelling abuse. Their flight is overbooked, and for a while it seems they're to be bumped, until Alex, one of the few people not shouting, takes a duty manager aside, disappearing beyond the damaged luggage counter. Denis looks almost on the verge of tears, to the point where Mikaël wonders if he should say something reassuring. When Alex returns, shaking hands with a different man, he has their boarding passes. There, put them in your pocket, he tells Denis. Go through and have a coffee or something, and call your mother when you land or I'll never hear the fucking end of it. Denis, only ten years or so Alex's junior, nods, nods, and heaves his overstuffed shoulder bag's strap over his head. Alex regards him a moment, then reaches into Denis's top pocket to remove the envelope containing their itinerary. Here, you take his, and he holds it out to Feliks, who takes it with a nod, open-jaw chewing.

Once through security, Alex gone, Mikaël, Feliks and Denis drink a Carlsberg each, leaning on one of the high tables outside a corporate chain bar. Barely a word is spoken.

It had seemed, initially, fairly exciting. Accompanying a director to LA for a funding expedition, he the driver and 'muscle' (though what muscle might be needed for on a funding expedition he didn't know), and he would make more money in four weeks than he had in six months in the army—not that that was much. Three months post-discharge and he'd mostly been kicking his feet at his aunt's house in Biryulyovo, manning the door of Alex's strip club once, maybe twice a week at most, which provided just enough money for groceries and beer. One night Hela had cornered him, drawn a line around his head with fine-topped marker. You're destined to travel, she'd told him, laughing, in the break between her lesbian-cowgirl showdown and the crotchless can-can climax, and she'd dotted a big dipper on one side of his buzzed scalp, black ink on bristles. Yeah, she'd said, I can already see you on the other side of the world. Hela's mother had read soldiers' fortunes for housekeeping back in Urdansk. Hela said her garters were hand-me-downs. She'd been in his maths class back in high school.

It was a pissing down Friday, half-empty of retired sailors, when Alex had called Mikaël into the heating flue cupboard that doubled as his office and told him he was going to Hollywood.

Alyana's fuckbrained son wants to make movies, he said, and shrugged as if he just didn't know what on earth the youth of today was coming to. I need someone to go over there with him and make sure he doesn't blow all my money.

It seemed like a good deal. Drive Denis the Fuckbrain around, take him to meetings with Alexei's contacts, make sure no half-baked silk-shirted Valley banjitskiys get any ideas about reinvesting the two million rubles Alexei had placed in a high interest savings account for fuckbrain's debut feature. Seed money, he'd called it. Mikaël didn't know what seed money was, but he knew how to deal with half-baked banjitskiys: one hand around the throat, one around the balls, and twist until either comes off. He imagined Valley banjitskiys as softer than the average, and easily squashable, like prunes.

But Alex hadn't said anything about low-ranking mafioso thugs coming along for the ride, which was obviously what Feliks was. Dragons and ships tattooed on the divots of his knuckles, an eight-pointed star right on his Adam's apple, rings thick as coins. Mikaël wouldn't be twenty for another month, but he'd known plenty of Feliks' sort. He'd seen one stamp on the trachea of a kid from his basketball team back in high school, in combat boots, out back of the Young Cadets centre, because the kids' ball had bounced into his legs, and he'd been two-thirds through a bottle of Kubanskaya on a chilly Sunday lunchtime and why the hell not. The kid's trachea made a sound like mud cracking on a frozen bog. The ball was Mikaël's.

The kid in the car rental service is giving them shit. A black kid with a pencil moustache and a little glittering cross in one earlobe. Yo they not my rules man, you got to have the docket. You know—docket? Mikaël's English is almost non-existent, and Denis is umming and forcing out broken sentences so riddled with pauses it seems like he's had a stroke. The LA sun is hidden behind a skirt of smog and cloud, the area around the airport a swathe of concrete.

Why are we listening to this chorn asshole? Feliks says in Russian. Ey! Chorn! he yells. The kid clicks his tongue and cocks his head, and Mikaël knows where this is headed. You don' give shit, Feliks says in heavily accented English, enunciating each word and pointing a gnarled finger, the last phalange of which skews downward as if it has been previously cracked, wrist chain dangling. Pff, don't point yo finger at me man, go see the office, see what they say, y'all need a docket, all they is to it. Denis is still speaking in slow motion: Ah... if want... but, no dock'tet... can? The kid shakes his head and cockeyes. *Dock*et man, docket, ain't no dock tit, and ain't no dock titties neither. Not tall, the kid is still half a foot taller than Denis.

It is 2005. It still sounds magical to Mikaël, like a year from the future. Before they left Moscow, he'd gone to Hela's place with a backpack filled with cured sausage and his mother's pasta salad, a bottle of vodka, and thrown stones at her bedroom window from the little parking lot out back of the concrete-clad five-storey mini-block behind a tallow factory where she lived. I have a doorbell! she yelled. Doorbells are for people who can't throw straight, he said, and held up the bottle and a sausage. Her hair was pushed back and mashed down in a thick crust of bleach, and she was pulling off a translucent glove finger by finger. I suppose you never thought to use a telephone either, mister romance? What, I'm not worth the price of a phone-call? Don't make a damn elephant out of a fly—can I come up or are you coming down? She tossed the cellophane glove over her shoulder and rested her chin on her wrists. Take your feet in your hands and go forwards.

Her place smelled of amonia, bath salts and her menthol cigarettes, and she was in loose flowing Chinese print pyjama shorts and a vest top that revealed her bra. They sat on her carpet, dipping the sausage into the pasta salad and drinking vodka from little tumblers, still sticky from sloppy washing. He told her about LA, hoping to detect a sign that she would miss him, or, at least, a sign that she would not miss him so he could stop fixating on her, but she remained, as ever, confoundingly ambivalent. The money sounds good, she said, scooping up a gob of pasta matter, but I wouldn't take any job from Alex. She shovelled in the gob and took a chunk off her sausage. Nearby, a neighbour was hollering along to their radio, some out-of-date ballad. That's dumb, he said, he's your boss. She shrugged as if that was the stupidest possible observation. That's different, that's his front business—and he does nothing, it's all Dora running everything, and if Dora tells you the way something is she gives you a tooth. How is it different? he said, emptying his glass and refilling. She shrugged, stood up from her cross-legged position, stretched her arms to the ceiling, turning her torso into something Mikaël had seen in black and white 'art' photos: nude warrior women on grey beaches, inhabiting bodies so shaped it made his cells vibrate. I wonder, he thought, what an extra-terrestrial would think of that kind of female body—would it be like him seeing a cow, or a porpoise? What do I care, she said, it's purple to me, and she nipped his earlobe with her thumb and forefinger as she padded barefoot to the tiny bathroom and began to run the squeaking, rust-encrusted shower.

Hela's nose was Roman or something—arching out, sloping down, and her neck was narrower than it seemed it should be, lean muscles on either flank of her throat, like

168

the neck of an older woman, as if she'd lost her baby fat whilst still a kid and grown lean and firm, probably from the dancing, and the late nights and vodka and cigarettes that go along with it, but she was still the most beautiful girl Mikaël had ever seen, even though he knew she also wasn't, not really, that it was more about the effect she had. But when you think about it, isn't that what people mean when they say that? Isn't that why it means something? Because of how they make you feel? Once he'd helped her sluice the thick, noxious paste from her hair and revealed the new vivid yellow-blonde, her head hanging upside down under the shower head and milky water flowing, he tousled her hair with a faded yellow towel, standing behind her, watching the two of them in the toothpaste-spattered mirror. So you think Alex is putting pasta in my ears? He's always putting pasta in someone's ears, she said, so if not yours then someone else's. Am I staying over? he said. She stopped towelling a moment and eyed him in the mirror. It's on the drum, she said, closing her eyes again.

Denis goes back towards the rental office, way on the other side of the parking lot, to see about a docket, leaving Mikaël with Feliks, who is staring openly at the black kid, his torso tense and puffed up, as the black kid busies himself a few cars away, polishing windscreens, returning Feliks' stare. Cut it out, Mikaël says. Feliks leans back against a Chevrolet, hands in pockets. Get yo ass off the car man, the kid calls out. Feliks mutters a slur, takes out a Pall Mall. Hey, Mikaël says, they'll call the cops you know. Yo! The black kid is pacing over to them now, slinging his polishing rag over his shoulder and swaggering as if he's thirty pounds bigger than he is. Yo man, don't lean on that car man. Hey— Mikaël tries again, but Feliks, eyes still locked on the kid, raises his hands in innocence and lifts his butt from the car's door. No problem, my nigger. The kid looks, for a second, as if he's been slapped, then as if the slap has left a toxic residue. What you say? he says. No problem, my nigger, Feliks repeats, loudly, patting the kid's shoulder, which fits almost completely in Feliks' gnarled, scar-tissued hand. He holds the pack of Pall Malls out to him. Want? The kid manages to realign himself, straightening out his spine as he takes half a step back. I see, I see, he says. Feliks shrugs, pockets the pack. No problem, my nigger, he says again, and takes a big drag, exhaled smoke curling into the humid, overcast air. Once the kid has left for the office he leans back on the Chevrolet, screws his cigarette out on the window glass and lights another. He offers the pack to Mikaël, which Mikaël accepts, watching the kid growing distant as he makes his way across the lot, his hip-rolling, straight-spined walk.

The next afternoon, after a night in a rented single-bedroom apartment, Feliks curled on a two-seater sofa, Mikaël on the floor with his backpack for a pillow, they drive to Culver City, Mikaël behind the wheel, Denis in back, Feliks with the passenger seat pushed back as far as it will go and his boots up on the dash, some local station playing hip-hop that Feliks

170

hums and grunts along to. The sun is sitting low in a hazy, suphuric sky, and Mikaël has the feeling of being far away from everyone who has ever really known him, as he merges onto the US-101. Denis is holding his script between his hands and peering solemnly at it as if it holds some ancient secret. What's it about? Mikaël asks, and Denis is slow to move his eyes from it and up to Mikaël's in the rearview. It's about Russia, he says, so slowly Mikaël wonders if something's wrong with him, mentally, like a handicap — there was a kid in school like that, who'd stare at you for seconds before he said whatever it was he had to say, and was always trying to hold people's hands. Mother Russia! Feliks blurts out, and turns it into a refrain to the rhythm of the electronic grind dispensed by the radio, clicking his thick thumbs and sucking his lips to make them pop. So why don't you just make it in Russia? Mikaël says, but Denis has retreated back inside himself.

When they get to the production company (a thick wooden door, as if to some exclusive secret garden, with a buzzer and a single, minute engraving declaring BRIGHT STAR FILMS), Denis's face looks like a taut mask, and his breathing has become loud and deliberate. When the female voice crackles through the intercom ('Hello', no question mark) he manages to croak out the name of Alexei's contact ('Dimitriy Borskov') and a noun ('meeting'). There is a brief crackly silence, before the intercom goes dead. Then: Um... okay, and a harsh hydraulic thunk releasing the door mechanism.

Inside, it's like the set of a 70s science fiction film, augmented by framed posters and the smell of heated milk. Feliks' boots clomp on the polished flooring. The receptionist, some mixture of single mother and fashion android, nods at them from behind a tall, gleaming desk, and disappears into one of the bright offices that adjoin the central skylit atrium. These cunts have money, Feliks says, fingering the waxy leaves of an aloe vera plant. Several minutes later, the receptionist emerges, glancing at them, returning to her desk, and an older woman, a producer of some sort Mikaël guesses, appears in the office doorway. Her billowy blouse is connected cuff to hip, creating something like wings. Gentlemen? she says, in what Mikaël thinks might be a British accent. Do you want to come in? Standing, straightening, Denis looks at Feliks. Stay here, he says, in Russian, and to cut off any reaction, have a coffee. Ah—he signals to the receptionist—coffee, coffee, and he points at Feliks, leaving the receptionist frowning, Feliks' boots up on an artisinal table. Come on, he says, nudging Mikaël.

So, says the producer woman, from behind a conspicuously organised desk, you're here to see Dimitriy? Yes, yes, Denis says, clutching his script. The office window looks out over a sun-baked parking lot fringed by graffiti murals and the backs of boutiques. The shelves are lined with books, DVD box-sets, ring-binders.

Right, the producer woman says, looking from Denis to Mikaël and back. Her skin is chestnut, decorated with dark freckles and sunspots, as if it wasn't always that way, and her desk displays two pictures of her with a pre-adolescent girl, no husband. Do you have a number for him?

Number?

A phone number. Can you call him I mean.

Denis pats his pockets as if to get out his phone, then says Ah, no. Don' have.

The producer woman nods. She opens a drawer, takes out a curled yellow Post-It. Would you try calling him for me? She hands the Post-It to Denis. He looks at the numbers. You wan'—

Just give that number a try for me, if you wouldn't mind.

She leans back in her seat, watching, flicking her eyes occasionally to Mikaël, as Denis dials. Mikaël can hear the extended *blee-bleep* of the no service tone. Not work, Denis says, handing back the Post-It.

Mm, she says. Then, sitting upright, How do you know Dimitriy?

Ah... he friend of... uncle.

The woman nods slowly. Well, I'm afraid Dimitriy left the company a few weeks ago.

Again, she looks from Denis to Mikaël, and back again, taking in their reactions. Denis' throat lets out a sort of murmuring noise. He leave?

He leave, yes. He left.

Denis nods, as if he understands, then: Where go?

She lets out a laugh, shifts in her chair, realising, perhaps, that Denis hasn't the faintest idea what he's doing. You tell me, she says finally.

He go? Mikaël says, the first thing he's said since the car.

She eyes him a moment. He go. No idea where. But—she pats a pile of scripts—he took thirty-two thousand dollars of the company's money with him. So we'd quite like a chat.

Look, she says finally, when Denis' silence and mutterings have convinced her of his uselessness, whatever you had going with Dimitriy, obviously not going to happen now, so. And there's an active police investigation, so if you hear from him you need to get in touch with us or the police, if you don't want to be charged as accessories, okay? She stands, preparing to shepherd them out. Denis, still seated, looking at his knees, holds out his script. Please, you read? he says.

Before the producer woman can turn her expression into an answer they hear clip-clopping footsteps approaching and the door swings open. Sorry Karen, the receptionist says, then to Denis, your associate needs to leave. Now.

As the weeks go by, Alex's list of contacts gradually implodes. There's the junior agent at United who turns out to be a mailboy; the independent producer who'd liquidated his production company so he could open a small alligator farm; the actor whose agent passed on the message that he didn't remember who Alex was and to stop calling; the actress who simply told them to go fuck themselves. The fee Alex was paying Mikaël was lump, and expected to cover a trip lasting a month, tops, but it had spiralled to almost that long already with no strong funding leads, and Alex had made it clear that if they came back without funding that was it for

Denis' 'career'. Their apartment had become truly awful: dirty clothes everywhere, take-out boxes still with week-old lumps of red pork rotting in oily slicks of sauce, empty bottles, full ashtrays, bottles-cum-ashtrays, pizza boxes-cum-ashtrays. Feliks had begun buying loaves of bread, tearing the cellophane bags open down the side, stuffing his face with ragged chunks then leaving the torn bag and half-destroyed loaf in a corona of crumbs on the kitchen work surface or the coffee table or the floor, and Mikaël was sure he'd heard rats, scruffling around in the night, just couple of meters or so from his spot on the floor. He would smoke out on the raised hallway, leaning on the railing and looking out over the two-tiered horseshoe of apartments off the Arroyo Seco Parkway, at the radon glow of the city radiating up into the night-orange sky, the slow progression of traffic circulating on towards Highland Park, Pasadena, Alhambra. Twice he called Hela, from the little tapered flip-top Nokia Denis had bought him on arrival (one for each of them), but he was never sure of the time difference, and she neither picked up nor called him back, and her texts were oblique, coming in the middle of the night and inviting no response.

Denis, it became clear, was something approaching an alcoholic. No raging, no flip-outs, just sad, constant drinking, which he'd try to hide from Feliks and Mikaël, pointlessly—pointless because it was obvious what was going on and because it assumed they might complain or intervene. Mikaël noticed him drinking in the morning—late morning, when they'd roused. He'd be in his room, taking nervous little hits from a hip flask whilst looking at himself in the mirror, holding quiet stop-start conversations with whatever it was he saw in there. By the time he emerged his small, boy-like face would be pale and wan and red at the eyes and ears, around his neck, and he'd be giving off this stale smell that put Mikaël in mind of garages, petrol. He'd sit at the small table by the window and gaze out at the passing traffic, whilst Feliks snored on the sofa, or practiced kick-boxing in his underwear, or masturbated in the bathroom. Why do you wanna make films anyway? Mikaël asked eventually, one midday, over instant coffee that tasted of boiled printer ink, and little flaky too-sweet breakfast cakes from a nearby 7/11. Seriously, I mean… they're just films. Denis just sighed, and kept on gazing out the window. From the bathroom, he heard the unmiskable sound of Felikx ejaculating into the sink.

In their second week in town, after striking out with almost every contact and after several mornings of humiliating, completely useless cold-calling, Feliks had insisted they all go out and get women. If I have to sit in that fucking apartment with you two miserable fucks one more night I'm going to rape one of you, he'd said, and then the other one, and Denis had laughed but it didn't seem to Mikaël like Feliks was joking. They walked along the side of North Figueroa, past strip malls and housing complexes, until they reached a parking lot surrounded on three sides by strips of shops, bars and take out places, settled themselves in at a place called the Three One One, drank beer under fairy lights as Feliks propositioned every pair or group of women who came in. He had the kind of musky, caveman bravado common to men like him: no shame, no self-control, no hesitation, not caring for one second if he repulsed anyone. A pair joined them: airport workers from LAX, one Lithuanian, one Venezuelan, both young and tired looking, particularly the Venezuelan. Probably not more than twenty-two, she looked like she was in the middle of some long period of convalescence: downsloping drifts under deep-set eyes. I work in the Quiznos, sometimes a pizza restaurant too, she told Mikaël, leaning into him to be heard over the too loud RnB, giving him a generous waft of her scent, of honey-ish perfume and sweat. She pronounced it Queeznoss, raystowrant. In what? Queeznoss—you know? The Lithuanian, mousey brown and tinted purple under the lighting, was laughing at Feliks' spiel, throwing her head back, play-slapping his chest. This one is trouble! she said to her friend. Feliks pulled her up to the dancefloor, and the Venezuelan took Mikaël's wrist. Dance? Denis, sitting next to them, had drifted into his head. No dance, Mikaël said, take him. Director! Denis, sleepy eyed, startled, clicked in—his face had a terrible resting melancholy. This chick wants to dance with you, Mikaël said in Russian, taking the girl's hand off his writst and guiding it over to Denis'. He director, film director—you like. The Venezuelan's face lit up with curiosity, and she persuaded Denis, still startled, to his feet, led him over to the dancefloor like she were some mother figure leading a little boy. Mikaël sat in the booth, drinking his Estrella, watching them on the little dancefloor, barely bigger than a lounge, some goatee'd guy behind a mixing desk queueing up tunes on CD and poking the air with one raised finger again and again and again, bobbing his neck, Feliks all over the Lithuanian like a starfish trying to swallow its prey, Denis jigging in uncomfortable slow motion as the Venezuelan shimmied and bogled. He slipped out when he could, walked back alone, along North Figueroa, only to remember that Feliks had the only key, so he went to the small, concrete-lined communal pool and lay on a lounger looking up at the impenetrable night sky: a murk of colour and non-colour, light pollution and air pollution, stretching up, up, to no visible stars. No—some were visible. He could see them when he relaxed his eyes. He woke up some time later, no hint of dawn yet, the smell of the pool treatment chemicals in his nostrils, walked up the stairs to the apartment and opened the door on Feliks and the Lithuanian rutting front to back on the sofa. He walked to the table, picked up his cigarettes, and went back to the pool.

Why do you let him talk to you like that? Mikaël asked Denis, the following afternoon. The women had gone, and Feliks, not unusually, had spent the morning in a state of hungover pique, snapping and digging at Denis. This place is a fucking hog's bathroom, why do I have to clean up everyone else's shit? Did you manage to find her cunt? Could you get your little thing in there, director? Did you like making with a spic chick? Did she taste spicy? Clean up the fucking kitchen, it reeks. Of course, most of the mess was his. But when Mikaël asked Denis why he didn't stand up for himself, he'd just look at his feet, or stare out the window, or mutter something about how he didn't mind, Feliks was just letting off steam, it didn't bother him. You're a coward, Mikaël told him. If you didn't take his shit, he wouldn't give it to you. Denis looked as if something under his face, some weight-bearing pillar, had just been cracked, and the colour drained, and he picked up his tumbler, still with a mouthful of vodka inside, and hurled it at the wall.

We've got one, Denis says, once he's off the phone. It is two weeks later, a month and change into their venture, and they haven't had a meeting for over a week. Mikaël is lying, shirtless, on the sofa, sucking the last life from a joint, Feliks out somewhere with one of the women he picked up in the days following his seal-breaking encounter with the Lithuanian. One what? Mikaël says. A meeting! Shit, shit. Denis' hands are shaking. He pours himself a drink, necks it. Relax, Jesus. Who's the meeting with? Denis just shakes his head 'don't know', looks at himself in the mirror. He has lost weight around the face since they arrived, gained around the hips. Mikaël sucks hot smoke and kills the joint.

They arrive, just the two of them, at a small off-yellow office block on a street of small office blocks in the Valley. There is no lobby—just a buzzer, and a glass door, and they're greeted by a sunburned man in boat shoes and cut-off jeans who introduces himself as Jason, shows them up to the second floor offices of XXSIX productions. It looks more

179

like the office of a not particularly successful opthamologist than of a production company, except the walls are lined with promotional materials from 1970s porn films: bouffanted vixens baring all but their nipples and genitals. Jason shows them into one of two small offices that branch off from the welcome room, where two further men are waiting: an older man with toad eyes and hairs coming from a large cheek mole, and a younger man, standing, arms folded behind his back, with thinning hair combed back and a forehead that looks dried out, like the skin has been pulled too thin across his skull. So, says the seated man in Russian, let me guess... you're Denis?

Denis nods. The standing man is looking at Mikaël. I'm the driver, Mikaël says, and Denis gives him a look.

I'll leave you comrades to it, says Jason, slipping back out into the welcome room.

Alex tells me you've got a script?

Denis nods, produces his script from his shoulder bag. Mikaël sees the title for the first time.

MAKING DINNER FOR ANDREI TARKOVSKY
by Denis Radchenko

And you're looking for...?

Around a million. It's in Russian and English, set in both countries. Russia and America I mean.

The man turns down his mouth as he nods. His accent is hard to place—not Moscow, anyway. Well, sounds great. I'm

180

sure it's great. I'll read it, of course.

But, it's not a porno, right? Mikaël says.

Denis nods. It's a kind of a... I don't know. A drama. With... I don't know, other elements.

The seated man waves his hands. We put money into all kinds of things, all kinds. We make adult entertainment, but we've invested in plenty of other projects. And, you know what, it's actually very good timing, because, believe it or not—the man gives a sort of performance of a disbelieving laugh—we're looking for a director. For one of our projects. Right Oleg?

The standing man nods.

And, you know, anything that can help out a friend of Alexei's, well... that's a bonus I say.

One of their younger directors, the man tells them, has dropped out of a project right before they're due to shoot. He got offered a job ADing a White Stripes promo that was too good to turn down, and has left them in the lurch. So you see, the guy says, it can work out perfectly. All Denis has to do, he tells them, is step in and fill the shoes of this flake, direct their film, which is due to shoot next week, and then, as long as that film isn't a total mess, they'll happily put a million dollars in to his project, providing the script isn't toilet paper.

In the car, Denis almost cracks a smile. Almost, but not quite. He stares out the window at the passing cars, the passing buildings, as radio voices blether in English between songs.

Mikaël wakes up on the lounger by the pool, his ears full of swirling water that deswirls and fragments into the usual soundscape, of sloshing pool and passing traffic szooshing on the Parkway. Except, there's something else—voices. Hyena cackle and footsteps, and he hears a woman, distant, calling words he doesn't understand, something like *Mai! Ma tee nee!* And then some panting creature is foot-falling past him, laughing, and

SPLOOSH

The giggling laugh disappears into the pool, then resurfaces, gasping for air, still giggling, splashing. In the moony glow of the poolside lights he can make out what seems to be a boy, bobbing up and down, smashing the water with his arms, apparently fully clothed, and the woman's voice

Wanchai! Tum arai?

He watches the woman run to the pool, a small, broad-shouldered, coffee-skinned woman in pyjama bottoms and a robe, black hair scooped back in a bun. She runs to the pool's edge. What are you doing? she gasps, in accented English. As Mikaël sits up on the lounger its slats creak, and she spins— rabbit in headlights. For a moment her mouth moves, as if to speak to him, but she doesn't. *Wanchai, mah tee nee!* But the boy is splashing, giggling, coughing water. He looks at least eight or nine, maybe older, but the sounds coming from his mouth have the high-pitched mania of a toddler. What's up? Mikaël says, rubbing the blur from his eyes, using one of the genuine American phrases he has learned. The woman, at least ten years his senior, takes him in. He need get *out*, she says. They use chemical—she pronounces it *ke-mi-kaw*—but he not unnerstan. Wanchai! Nahm mai dee! Mikaël takes off his t-shirt (the woman looks), his boots, his socks. He removes his wallet and flip-top Nokia and loose change from his pockets. He lowers himself into the chemical-smelling water, jeans clinging. He wades towards the boy. Come on, he says, in Russian, as he wraps his arms gently around the flailing creature, your mama's worried about you. The boy's manic delight switches to screeching resistance for a moment, but then, miraculously, he seems to calm into Mikaël's embrace, the writhing limbs slowing, his slim arms pressing into Mikaël's chest, his legs kicking without real force into his abdomen, until he has the boy at the shallow end steps, and his mother takes him by the arms, pulls him out, and the calm switches again to screeching. Wanchai! she yells, exasperated. Stop! Mikaël watches as the woman slaps the boy on the back of the hand. *Mai!* Again. *Mai!* The boy's screeches turn to wails, tears filling his eyes. Hey, Mikaël says, hey— he steps in. Listen, he says in English.

Her name is Mumii, she tells him, in her kitchen, in her apartment, on the ground floor of the two-tiered horseshoe, and she is Thai, her son half-American, his father not in the picture. He feels some English skill returning, but hers is significantly better. They talk about the boy, Wanchai, about his problems, Mikaël understanding less than half, sipping fridge-cold Coors Light under a flickering strip light. She is uncommon-looking, this woman—the frame of a boxer, but slim, a round face with a flat nose, something puppyish about her features, her full wide lips, and in her loose sleeping vest she is beautiful, vulnerable, unornamented. He thinks about trying to kiss her. You're a daddy? she asks. No. I had brother, same Wanchai. Same? she asks. Mikaël nods. Same. But... he die. He doesn't have the words to tell her in English what happened, so he tells her in Russian, and she listens, nodding as he speaks, as if she understands every word. When he wakes up, on her sofa, he isn't sure where he is for a moment, but then he remembers, and realises that the warmth he can feel pressed onto him is her, squeezed up, loose mouth pooting out sleeping breaths. Her smallness fits his rangey frame as if she'd always been there.

In the army, he'd been a Private First Class, stationed at Mitrovica during the last days of Russian involvement in Kosovo, enlisting when he was seventeen and lying about his age. He was inches taller than most, but lean—room on his frame for more muscle, and as he went through the training programme so he started to grow, laterals fanning out, little hard biceps ballooning, the lines of his abdomen hardening. He didn't have to do much, it seemed, to make the gains, as if his body had been primed and ready to expand for years. The recruits played their games—wrestling matches in the mud pit round back of the mess, bare-knuckle fights with a book kept for bets, beatings after lights out for the slow, the lazy, the stupid. Sergej, a lumpen sadsack from Kazan, took the worst of it, sacks of rocks into his gut, so bad he lost one of his kidneys. Mikaël did nothing to protect Sergej from the others, found he didn't really want to—he deserved it. He was useless.

Being stationed in Mitrovica was like being stationed on a farm back home: maintaining road blocks, building barricades, checking papers, assisting ethnic Serbs. Like being a traffic cop, with an AK47 slung over your shoulder. Occasional alerts about Albanian extremists, occasional run-ins with the arrogant, lazy French troops, the stoic, friendly Danes, the smarmy, polite British. There'd been a Serbian girl—Vesna. He'd been there at a checkpoint when her father brought ham and bread and cheese and hot pepper jam for the soldiers, and he'd offered her a smoke. She was tall and slender—taller than a lot of the soldiers, with a sort of clumsy arm-swinging grace, fair brown hair tied back showing her long, pretty neck. She took him to her father's barn, after dark, laid down blankets, brought meat, stone casks of home-brewed rakija. He found her body after a grenade was lobbed into a café off the main square—a few dead, a few with skin torn from flesh, with shrapnel gouged into legs. One of Vesna's legs was gone from the knee down, and part of her face. He had another fourteen months of service after that, checking papers, building walls, raiding private residences for Albanians, going with the others to the little smoky brothel above a hole-in-the-wall bar. Every now and then there'd be disagreements with the other troops, stand-offs—French or British guns at the other end of a mud road, terse discussions between envoys, the possibility of being the men to start World War III. He was moved to Pristina airport, put in charge of baggage checks. When his two years were up he felt as if he'd been a clerk in an unusual office, or a day labourer, both of which paid more. He'd grown a couple of inches upwards, several inches outwards, watched his body develop. No-one messed with him the whole time, even though he was quiet, undemonstrative. There was, he concluded, something about him. There had to be.

In the morning, once the paunchy Latina neighbour has collected Wanchai, he offers to drive Mumii to work. It's still early, the highway filling up with traffic, the soupy morning light struggling through the smog. In the distance, he can see the Hollywood sign—small, weird, unimpressive, gimmicky. She talks at him in English. He nods, listens, murmurs. He finds words he'd forgotten coming back to him. Why you come here? Why LA? He doesn't fully understand her answer—something, he thinks, about 'hope'.

They arrive at the location shoot a little late—a snippy woman with a walkie-talkie asks who he is. He's friend, Mumii says, and he is made to sign a form on a clipboard and pin a GUEST badge to his t-shirt. Is cool, huh? she says. Is my first job in LA. She goes to wardrobe, to make-up. She's given a leather jacket, skin tight jeans that aren't jeans—lycra really. So you can kick, she says, and thrusts her foot out at head height, holds it there, mock scowling. What you think?

She was, it turns out, a soldier too, back in Thailand—and then a security guard, and then a TV extra, and then a TV ass-kicker in the background of some period-set historical fight-fest. The make-up ladies have done a bang-up job—a weeping cut above her eye, swollen bruised jaw. Are you next? one of them asks him, before she sees the guest tag. He watches her fight, roll, spin, kick air. A wooden beam is broken over her head, and she tumbles backways like a puppet with its strings cut. He watches the men fighting—smaller than him, but more squat, little bulging musclemen, the way men are here: gym-sculpted. They stagger backwards, baby giraffe, wildebeest kneed, they flip, tumble, oomph, roll. Afterwards, they high five, whoop, holler, hug Mumii. He looks around the set: no AK47s, no garter belts. Pretty, fresh-faced girls and chuckling guys, sleeve tattoos, danish. He pictures himself amongst them, muscles built up, double their size, super-hero size, play-scuffling with Mumii, bringing home danish wrapped in napkins for Wanchai. I swiped you a cherry-custard, he'd say. Don't tell your mom. He would say it the American way. Mom.

He drives her home as the sun is setting, her hand resting on his knee like a wife's on a husband's. They collect Wanchai from Maria's place, calm and peaceful—he says a shy 'I like you' to Maria, eyes on the floor, as he leaves, and she coos, awws. Mikaël remembers his brother, before he died, how the only one he'd hug was their mum, back before the accident took them both away. They watch TV together, the three of them, Wanchai sitting on the floor and holding his socked feet in his hands, Mumii squeezing Mikaël's arm or knee or flank and throwing cheeky smiles at him, and once Wanchai has been put to bed—after tears and a tantrum, forced teeth-brushing, Mumii holding his head still with one hand and scrubbing his teeth with the other as he wailed and moaned — she takes Mikaël to her bedroom and takes off her clothes. Her body is strong, scarred — white rips in the flesh around her shoulder, high on her arm. His father? Mikaël asks. She shakes her head. My dad, and grandad. She starts to take his clothes off, but he pushes her onto the bed. She crawls back, coquettish performance, which he stops by placing his hands on her knees, and he tells her in Russian his plans for her before kissing his way up from the thick brown ankles. Her thighs could be a man's, but smooth — they shiver and tense as he tastes them.

He doesn't usually remember his dreams, but this one wakes him up in the dead of night and stays there, hanging like a tarpaulin over his half-awake mind. He is enormous, bulging, a planet-sized man, dragging the moon. He drags it everywhere he goes, the rope digging so deeply into the muscle of his shoulder that it hacks away the flesh, the sinue, digs its way into bone, and still he drag-drag-drags this moon, over some celestial desert, glittering night sands, dragging, up a never-ending dune — and there's a rap

RAP — RAP

at the moon at the

RAP — RAP! Mikaël!

at the door, at the

RAP RAP! Ey! Asshole! RAP

Too late — she's awake, lifting her face, face-down, from

the pillow, saying

Tum arai?

\peach\

WAKE up, we're dreaming!

We're not dreaming, this is real.

...It's real?

A ray's belly like an outstretched hand arcs through the blue. A dream of cone jellies tumbles.

Don't be such a baby Ping, of course it's real. He kicks my foot with his, but his heart's not in it. He's caught up in the dream.

We've been here an hour already. Busan Sea Center, an underground grotto by the beach. We've lost Peach. Our movie star babysitter, disappeared among the fishes. But you can't show panic—got to mind your little brother, keep him calm. You're the momma now. When Peach told us

Alright kiddoes, get your jackets, we're going on an adventure!

my stomach did a flip. His face is a poster. He seems to be blurred round the edges, like when you try to look at a lightbulb. I'd asked him earlier

What's it like being famous?

and he put an arm around my shoulder, and I died seven hundred electric deaths in a second, and he said

Why don't you tell me in seven or eight years when you're on every magazine cover, little superstar.

and he squeezed my shoulder. And then I was mad at him, and I didn't know why.

Deep within the tank is a shark. You can see him, swerving slowly in there, but he's too far away, just a shape really, bent by the glass. Occasionally you can see a little black eye or a blur of teeth. Ping's hypnotic state is starting to weaken. Where'd he go anyway?

I told you, he had to make a phone call. Movie stars have a lot of business.

But he's been gone forever n'ever.

Well, then I'm in charge. You want some snacks?

He side-eyes me. *You* don't have snack money.

Do too, Peach gave me some. You don't want any I'll just get some for myself.

Okay! I want Doritos.

Wait here. I mean it.

Okay. The red Doritos!

He presses his face up against the glass, squishing his button nose, to eye a passing barracuda. The enormous sunfish floats like a bad joke.

The halls are a spaceship, blue-dim and hushed, background muzak. People pass but no Peach. I used to watch him, on TV, under my covers, as he skulked around breaking hearts. A heavy man gives me a funny look. I find a passing uniform woman. Excuse me, I say in English, I can't find my dad. I don't know how to say 'movie star babysitter' in English. But the woman scare-eyes me and waves her hands, says something in Korean. I use the one Korean sentence I learned:

Yeongeo haseyo?

(Do you speak English?)

But she recoils again, shakes her head so violently it kind of weirds me out. She looks mad, or terrified, I can't tell, and skitters away from me like a cat from something scary. I don't get this place—grown-up adults skittering away from twelve-year-old girls like they're a demon spirit because they don't want to face the humiliation of being out-Englished. It's actually not great for a twelve-year-old girl's self-image you know. But hey, what's new—an adult putting themselves before the kid right in front of them? Tell me one I don't know. I wish I'd never come to this stupid country.

I lied—it's not the only sentence I know in Korean. I know plenty, that's just the only one I know spoken instead of sung. I know

If I let go of your hand, you'll fly away and break

and

You shine in this pitch darkness

and

We're the two who found our destiny

and a hundred more. I'd dreamed of riding bubble clouds over Seoul, in the arms of J-Hope. It was why I asked our father.

Can we come with you to Korea? Pleeease?

He'd looked at me, and said something about how he'd be working the whole time, but I begged and begged and begged, I hugged him and moaned, called him Big Poppa Elephant like he likes. And he said

Okay, okay.

if Ping agreed, and I knew I could make him. And then we flew here, from Bangkok, the three of us, and I didn't know why I'd wanted to come or what I'd hoped for. Father sat in the chair by the window with his glasses on reading through some script, making notes with one of his father pens (strictly off limits) while cloudscapes rolled past, and Ping fell so deeply open-mouthed asleep you'd've thought a spell had been cast on him.

Want to see my camera?

I look up. It's the heavy man. He's next to me, camera around his neck. He looks Chinese but speaks English, and there's something funny about his voice, like his tongue is too big for his mouth. He turns the camera to me, starts scrolling through images: close up on octopus bellies, suckers, a ray's weird eyes breaking the reflective surface of the water.

Wow, I say.

They're cool, he says flatly, scrolling. He's moved kind of close to me.

You looking for?

For my... my dad. Well—no, my dad's friend.

Dad friend? His face is strange—something strange about

it. I saw him, over there, I show you. He takes my hand in his firmly, starts to walk me toward the Amazon tanks, where we saw the giant weird bulbous things that looked more like monsters than fish floating along in greenish water.

You don't know what he looks like, I say, as he walks me.

I show you, I show you.

No-one knows who Peach is in Korea. In Bangkok he's on subway posters, he's all my friends talk about. He's a dream, they say, he's perfect, sooo handsome, sooo cute, and they're right. The upturned lip, the sweep of not-quite-messy hair. The first time dad said he was shooting a movie with him, I thought I was going to faint.

But no-one in Korea knows. He walks around, and they think he's a normal guy, just ten thousand times more beautiful, and rich. In the queue to pay for entrance, he was distracted, on his phone, as if he was mad at us, at me and Ping. I wanted to vomit. My mouth filled with spit. Thanks for taking us, I said, my voice coming out all quiet. Yeah, well, thank your dad, he said, not looking at us. But then he did look, and he rubbed the top of my head, and I wanted to dance and cry. I wanna see the octopus, Ping said. There was a huge octopus on the sign advertising the place. That might not be an actual octopus that they actually have you know, Peach said. It is too, I've seen it. I just wanted Ping to shut-up and stop making us both look stupid, but I couldn't kick him in front of Peach, so instead I poked Peach's stomach, on his t-shirt, on one of the little cartoon faces swirling over his flat tummy, and gave him a closed-mouth smile, and he said I was "alright".

I'm alright.

I am alright.

I let it loop around in my head as he paid for our tickets— the most beautiful beautiful boy. I'm alright. I am alright.

The heavy Chinese man has his hand around my wrist. He's smiling whenever he looks back.

I show you, over here, he says.

I find my head has gone blank, and my body is letting him pull me along.

But— you don't—

I show you.

The Amazon giants are floating, suspended, and we're passing groups of people, but no-one is stopping us, and my mouth isn't working. I'm watching it happen to another girl. This other me girl. She surprises me with how young she looks, younger than I feel, her little wrist tiny in the heavy man's heavy hand. When the man has turned into an unfamiliar dark corridor and then into an unfamiliar dark room, the girl decides to scream. But nothing really comes out. He's still saying things, the heavy man, some things in English, some in Chinese, and the girl, the me girl, tries to scream again, and gets closer, so the heavy man puts a hand over her mouth and says

shhhhh

and something about the way he says this with these big

panicked eyes looking right at me, me, kick-starts the thrump
of my heart, *my* heart, and I scream

HELP

and kick kick, and slip slip

and hallway, and running

and Amazon giants

and families milling

and run run run

until the girl, me

stops in the hall of the sharks.

And there they are: hovering in the dim

like dogs, mouths hanging open

with rows and rows

and rows of teeth

and the little black eyes that don't seem to see a thing.

I find my way back to the viewing room, but Ping isn't there.
Empty benches, Americans. I've killed my brother.

PIIING

I yell, and all the adults look. The rays are gliding past.

PIIING

I yell in the spaceship hall. I've lost my brother. He's with
the heavy man. I've killed my brother dead. I can feel a girl
crying, feel a girl's chest heaving, feel the waves washing over
a girl, like as if she's deep underwater, and the faces around
a girl are not kind, are not warm, and no-one is helping a girl.
Peach's attention had drifted once we were inside, amongst
the tumbling jellies and the terrapins. He'd kept up the

warmth as far as the octopuses, and Ping's disappointment that the giant on the sign was actually the size of two hands. And then he'd drifted, and drifted, until he wasn't there anymore—a girl had tried to stop it, making jokes for him and cutesie faces, like father likes, but no dice, and maybe he'd said something to a girl like how something had come up and he needed a girl to be in charge, and maybe he'd kissed a girl on her head before he'd gone. But what does it matter now, when Ping is being killed by the heavy man and a girl is at the bottom of the ocean? But Ping isn't dead—can't be, because that's him over there, holding the hand of a uniform woman, face all wet and tugged, and he's pointing a finger at a girl.

Maybe this is a dream, Ping says.

Maybe, a girl says.

The uniformed staff are hanging around, muttering in Korean. Out the glass front doors of the lobby they're closing up for the night, turning tourists away with shakes of their hands and heads. The beach trees are shifting in the breeze, broken-branched from yesterday's storm.

Soon, a girl's father will walk through the glass doors, hands in pockets. He'll charm the uniforms, slip them a tip. He'll say he's already arranged to have Peach killed, and Ping will smile, because he doesn't know any better. He'll take Ping and a girl for fancy gelato, which the girl won't want, because she'll be so exhausted she'll just want to curl up in bed forever, and her stomach will be small and shrivelled as a nut. He'll look at a girl, taking her in, give up on the jokes.

Ping will eat and eat, slurping up his treat, but a girl's father will continue looking at a girl, like she's a puzzle, trying to figure her out, and the girl will let the minutes of the night wash over her, like the minutes of a dream, the way she has taught herself to do when nothing is okay, and there's no way to make it okay, and there's nowhere else for her to go.

\dana carvey\

SO I'M sitting on the L-shaped sofa with Rufus, his bare feet in my lap for a foot rub (it calms him), and we're watching SNL clips, via YouTube, on the big TV, via Amazon Fire, and first of all I'm struck, still, by how weird and futuristic this is, how we're basically like a single mum and son from an unusually domestic episode of Star Trek or something, talking into our tricorders as Computer serves up the ship's entertainment package, and I'm on the verge of tipping over into melancholy about this—the death of analogue, of celluloid, the digital homogenisation of everything, the aesthetic and cultural holocaust that you're not meant to talk about—when Ru asks:

Who's that?

He's pointing at Dana Carvey, as George H.W. Bush. So I tell him.

He's hilare, he says, kicking his feet for attention. I give their soft undersides a good squeeze.

He is, I say, he was great. Really funny impressions.

Can we see some?

Do you think we can actually watch the end of something for once?

He huffs, and sulks, but only for play, and as the Bush clip ends we skip to impression clips: there's one of him prancing around on Leno, mid-90s, doing push-ups on the studio floor like the class clown performing at a party for the jocks, then going into voices. This is so *old*, Ru says, and he's right really. It looks ancient, from another time: grainy, strobey, smudged colours, weird lighting, weird hair, bad jeans. This must be for him how it was for me looking at black and white pictures of World War 2. As I got older, and filled in my visual memory banks, my worldliness, I became able to see the men behind the antiquity in those pics—behind the old haircut, the picture grain, I could see them, alive, as if they were right next to me. Could see what type they were (joker, josher, no-nonsense, dickhead), could almost hear them speak. But Rufus isn't there yet—Dana Carvey on NBC from 1994 is like the wreck of the Titanic to him.

What's he doing now? he says. If he's still alive.

Of course he's alive! He's about my age for God's sake. But then we look, and he's sixty-two. Garth is sixty-two.

Fuck, I say.

Oi! He hits me.

Sorry, sorry. Bloody hell though. Hard to believe, that.

Why? He reaches for his phone, attention drifted just enough, and I want to slap it away from his hand, stop him vanishing. Even if he only disappears into that poisonous thing for a few seconds, he always comes back less him. But we made an agreement. He's old enough to monitor his own usage, we agreed. Give them agency and guidance, the books say, and the books are usually right.

I should show you Wayne's World, I say. Up for a bit of

Wayne's World?

What's that? he says, in the screenglow, dabbing limply, in a way that makes me want to scream.

So we put on Wayne's World. To me it has the fingerprints of an SNL spin-off movie all over the opening, but he's lapping it up, and soon so am I: it's all so my youth. The font, the tunes, Stan Mikita's donuts, the mirth mobile. Wayne says hi to Old Man Withers, and I tell Ru it's a Scooby Doo reference. Wha? he says, no T, and I tell him to just wait, it'll pay off. And then he's headbanging along with Wayne and Garth to Bohemian Rhapsody (one of his favourite songs—if I've given him anything, it's a thorough grounding in the classics) and I'm thirteen again, in the passenger seat of my dad's Vauxhall, on the way back to mum's house after one of his weekends, in that strange spell when they were separated without the divorce, before they were reunited without the joy. And then I'm sixteen, on the sofa of my L-shaped bedroom, wrapped up with Nicky Alexander, watching the sequel, Kim Basinger doing her thing.

Take me, Garth.

Where? I'm low on gas and you need a jacket.

But then she pounces, and Garth goes all Hephner, bubble pipe and smoking jacket.

Nicky, Nicky—thee sweetest lad, the loveliest first, his body this nascent collection of bells and ropes. I'd see him years later, on the street—sure it was him, holding hands with some pinch-mouthed harridan who looked like her frown could strip paint. Whatever happened to *my* Nicky I wonder, the wise-cracking, shy/confident, big-handed drop-D power chord thwacker, the first boy who ever showed me love? Maybe the only one who ever really did. My mind does its tromboning thing as I realise how old I am now, my baby boy only a handful of years younger than I was then, and the West Sussex night out beyond the French doors seems stranger, longer, deeper, colder, the way it does when Ru has disappeared to bed and it's just me and the TV and a bottle of Tesco generic French Red.

The next day, Sunday, we put the sequel on, me and Ru. I'd forgotten almost all of it. Aerosmith, Garth's pubes, Tia Carrera's ridonkulous hotness. I remember the brief, weird fling I'd had with a Hong Kongese doctoral student, a few years after Ru'd been born and his dad had been told to fuck off and I'd begun to Rediscover myself; how intense and clingy and broken and sexy she'd been, how I'd enjoyed her body more than her, how I'd ended up running away from her as fast as I could, slightly terrified of the unknown direction life might've been heading. We watch Wayne's vision-quest with Jim Morrison (Ru, God bless him, notes the out-of-date racial element of the Naked Indian), their impromptu YMCA performance (Is this homophobic? I wonder outloud, and Ru says I don't think so, and he's probably right, which makes my heart just want to starburst), Garth's cherry-popping at the hands of Kim Basinger. And the whole lovely hour or two is a frothy concoction of togetherness and laughter with the boy who turned out to be the love of my life. The other boy, the Nicky boy, hangs around in my thoughts. And there's this undercurrent, this sadness or something, from who knows where—life been lived? Memories held at arm's length? But when isn't there these days? And when it's over, I look out the French doors at the garden fences, backs of houses. There's nothing out there at all, I used to think, back in the day, for so much of my life. But there is.

YOU'RE A BOY,

twenty-two, and you have no idea who you are. Geek boy/ rock star? Handsome/chugly? You've played a great many roles already. You wander foreign streets. Jacobs University Bremen. Wander halls, subterranean housing, josh in bars, hone your flirt, your English, your German. Here's a thought experiment, your logic professor says, in Rajahstani-flavoured English, in the middle of Lower Saxony, to a lecture theatre of junior globe trotters, imagine you're a very particular barber. You shave every single person in your village who never shaves themselves, and you never shave anyone who does shave themselves. But! Your wife is expecting you for dinner! And oh my, a five o'clock shadow! He draws a stubbled, troubled face on the triple whiteboard. Do you shave yourself? Can you? If you do—poof! You don't exist— you can't shave a self that shaves itself. If you don't—poof! You don't exist. You must shave every non-shaver. So—how on earth are you meant to meet your poor wife?

You take your DSLR out on the town. Videographer in training, you tell the British girl, the one full of bold fragility, who emerged through the dim crowds of Danny's Rockbar like a spell. You take it out *drinking*? she slurs. It's insured!

you yell in her ear, over the middle eight of Enter Sandman. You take her to bed (single bed, Krupp college halls), dab at each other, play on each other, eyes too blurred for contact, like looking through a cataract. You think she comes but it's hard to tell. She won't last long anyway this one—her bruises frighten you. When she needs to go to hospital, even though it's baffling, you stay with her. This is the kind of man(boy) you are. You are not what they said you were back in Aarhus—Birgitte, Luna, the man playing your father. You're proving that.

You're a big city man(boy), cutting a swathe through Copenhägen with your camera bag. In the gym mirrors you see what others fail to see, as you tear and rip and fill in the spaces with more you: you see the old lines, what you used to be. On music video sets, calf tattoos displayed by cargo shorts, you become this other self, constructed self: a new locus of self. You party like a motherfucker. The coke turns out to be ketamine. You drag yourself off the bathroom floor. Your dick goes soft. Kitten girls nuzzle at the ankles of this you-suit, stroke its shapes. It's about types, your professor had said, another time, another day, morning, rainy, in a basement level seminar room in the bowels of an eighties build, it's about how, in any system, any term you can usefully employ has a type. Natural numbers, for example. What I *want* you to be thinking about, he said, is how this relates to *you*. *Does* it relate to you? You mean, what kind of type am I? you'd said. No, exactly *not* that, he'd said, smiling, and the others had laughed. I mean: what *happens* to you, whatever you is, when you begin to view yourself in terms of a type? You busked some kind of answer you can't remember, for the benefit of the girls who were present, but you remember the way your professor regarded you, with one of those looks you found impossible to read.

I just think, ah, this is an incredibly exciting and interesting project, you tell the funding commission. I think it's a beautiful script and an important story. I think it should be told. But why are you the one to tell it? asks the woman doing the impression of his mother. You let the images from the script float back to you: the mutated manboy, the head like the moon. That'll require some serious prosthetic—you have no idea how that works. Well, you say. I understand. I understand what it's like. Go on, the mother woman says. Dazzle us.

You see the actor losing it. Under the prosthetic his eyes, so expressive, have escaped him. Come on man, he needs a few minutes, Jesus, says the actress. She has a tender beauty the likes of which you've never seen, and a husband you would like to be. Whad're we gonna do? your 1st AD asks. You have two ADs on this shoot. You've never had one before. Ah... I mean give him a break, right? Can we take twenty minutes? You see him eye the 2nd AD, poker-faced, as if you've confirmed something about yourself they'd been waiting for you to confirm. I think we're done for the day, the 2nd AD says, more past you than to you. When the make-up team go to remove the prosthetic they find the actor gone. What do you mean gone? With it on? Gone where?

You have lost control of the project, your first funded project, the project that will make or break you, that will set up forty years of a directorial career or a life drifting here and there for scraps. You are confirming all they said and thought about you. Henning Henning Shit His Pants, Henning Skousen, little piggy, piggy titties, little shitball Henning, ball of shit. Always selfish, always messing up, only think of yourself, no discipline, can't you think of your mother for once? No intelligence, no patience. Little shitfuck, fat fuck Henning, roll him in lard and fry him up like Spam! Spamning, Spamenning, Spam boy! You're dead inside, you're empty inside, aren't you, little nothing, standing there, you're not *my* son, who's responsibility are you anyway? Mine? I gave up everything when I had you, and this is how you repay me? I was a young girl, I had plans you know, are you even grateful? Are you? But he's back, the actor. Next afternoon, on set. Sorry about yesterday, he says, and the Writer is hovering nearby holding a steaming paper cup of tea. Things just... got to me a bit. Personal things, y'know? Won't happen again. Hey, man, you say, and put your hand on his shoulder—the first time you've touched him aside from a handshake, your work is incredible. I mean it. Yesterday is yesterday. Now we have two more shoot days and no budget for reshoots. I need you. He looks at you, this older man, like a student at a teacher. Gimme today's pages, he says, and let's get that fucking head back on me. The Writer is watching with something like half of half a smile, dim moons under his eyes.

You're an LA man, man—lettin' it aaall hang loose bay*bee*!

You know how to schmooze the schmoo, and schmooze you do, and before long you're helming a psychological thriller. You've been warned about the Teenage Actress. Crazy. As. Fuck. But hey, slip her half a foot of premium Danish sausage, maybe that'll calm her down, am I right? Dude they aaalways wanna play with the director, are you kidding me? S'like taking candy from a baby, bay*bee*! And *she's* been down to play since she was in *braces*, tellin' you, *not* a choir girl. You find her hard to get to, hard to grasp—an assistant girl always keeping you, and everyone else, at arm's length. You manage to get her and the male lead to your place for a read-through, but something's wrong. It's dead. Lumpen. Listen, you say, when the catalogue model-handsome, GI Joe-handsome actor has stepped out to make his thousandth phone call, and you can feel that familiar feeling of it all slipping away, I really need there to be a dynamic between you two, you know? Uh-huh, she's saying, eyeing her script. You notice little droplets of wine-coloured blood at a hangnail she's still picking. You look out onto your balcony, where the mannequin-faced actor is remonstrating, phone to ear. You feel okay about him? you ask. Her eyes flash up at yours. Yes. Fine. It's just, you start, it's coming across so... I'll fix it, she says, her mouth jumping into a smile. When you run it again, there's a spark of life. Some kind of something. She nuzzles her head into his chest, squeezes his arm, and when she looks up at him there's something... fear? Raw— if he notices he fails to react, but that could work for his character, and he's switched on his butter-honey voice. Three bottles have been emptied by the time

211

he departs in an Uber, and there's a pleasant looseness over everything. You see her rubbing her eyes. Tired? She kind of laughs. So, where are you from again? You tell her about Aarhus. Tell her about the river behind uncle's barn, where your sister fell in, how she'd spent a week in the children's unit at Skejby Sygehus and lost three frostbitten toes. You feel there's an understanding between you, a bond—feel your teenage heart thrumping in your twenty-nine-year-old chest. Twenty-nine—where did the years go? When she is underneath you, you have the strangest sensation: as if you're floating just above the surface of an undulating midnight ocean, looking in. I guess we shouldn't've done that, you laugh, lighting up one of the pre-rolleds you keep by the bed. It's fine, she says. You find yourself unsure how to read almost everything she says.

When they take the film away from you, a week before the shoot is due to finish, they tell you it was a bad fit. You'd felt, in the previous three weeks—half of the shoot—something akin to your skin being on fire. Like a thrumming cascade of concomitant panic attacks. You'd spent your off hours pacing in tight circles around your sofa, sleeping for an hour before waking with the fangs of acid reflux shredding the tail of your oesophegus, then dry-puking little poisonous slicks of bile. The set, with its constellations of cast and crew, its floating clouds of power and influence, its cliques of craftsmen and labourers, the semi-sexual mania hanging over it all, had begun to seem like some kind of gargantuan alien body, with you, ant-like human, stuck at the feet, gazing up at the head, which, you would suddenly remember, was you! And then the dizzying vertigo, the nausea, as you were catapulted from foot to head, plonked atop the behemoth, made to plot its course, which you were meant to have planned already (it being assumed that you are, of course, an expert in behemoth course plotting). The Teenage Actress, who you'd thought you might have been in love with, had not made eye contact with you for several weeks, and whilst her performances remained strong, even brilliant, she had begun shutting herself in her trailer immediately before and after each scene, or else she would fade somehow into the bowels of the set, whilst the News Anchor-handsome actor began to develop what seemed to be a genuine and passionate hatred for you. By the time you noticed—actually noticed, as if stepping outside your body and looking at yourself—that your coffee intake had quintupled, that your sleep had become almost non-existent, that you'd ploughed through a dimebag of sinsemilla (which would usually last you a month) in close to a week, that you hadn't looked at your storyboards since the second week, and that you hadn't exchanged a word with either your lead actress or actor outside shooting since the third week, it was clear that you had lost the film. You'd had it—it had been yours, your name on the poster, bound for festivals, awards... and then it wasn't.

Your agent tells you it's not the end of the world, that this kind of thing happens all the time—part and parcel of the business. There isn't a soul in town who won't understand this, he tells you, an' if there is? Fuck 'em! You're still getting a paycheque my friend. You don't know at this point that you won't work again for half a decade.

When Johan Beck kills himself, you are in an AirBnB in Joshua Tree with two models-slash-actresses and Jared, the guy from your gym who supplies your steroids. You see the news on your cellphone:

DANISH DIRECTOR FOUND DEAD IN LAS VEGAS HOTEL ROOM

For a disturbing, tromboning moment, the director is you.

You have gone to Vegas (Jared *had* suggested this), not Joshua Tree, and you have killed yourself.

And you are not in Joshua Tree now — what is Joshua Tree anyway? Look out the window: it's an alien landscape out there, barren and lifeless, stretching to sand-blown nothing, and so hot it's clearly not habitable by humans.

No, you are not in any National Park — you are in fact not you, but whatever remnant of self is left, catapulted outwards, when you kill yourself in a Vegas hotel room. And look, out on the covered patio: see the succubi lounging by the muscle-bound demon under the blow of the wall-mounted fan. Whatever remnant of self is left, that's you, in this empty oven-hot limbo, in an air-conned bungalow, gazing into the sapphire-silicon hand-window to read of your own death.

But it is not your death — remember your name? There — feel it float down to inhabit you again. Johan Beck was forty-two years old, and leaves behind an ex-wife, the actress

Sara Beck, and no childen. His death is not being treated as suspicious. The actress Sara Beck, who you directed, who made you feel like a child, with her beauty, her warmth, her tender care for that troubled actor, on that set, of that short, that strange short, your first set, a million years ago. You'd seen most of Johan's films, bought his band's first two albums. You'd wanted very badly to be him.

But the others, who are not demons, will not know who he is, and you do not have the energy to explain. Fix a jug of caipirinha. Bring it out to the patio. The desert heat will envelope you, but it's tolerable, even pleasant, in the shade, with the fan. Look at the lines of the raven-haired one, the soft firmness of her tan midriff as she lies with her head on the lap of the blonde. Listen to Jared's stories, that backtrack and skip lanes and end up where they started. Look out over that empty, alien landscape. It's not alien, in fact: it's Native American. Serrano. That oven-empty landscape is the bed of a blood ocean, and this fenced yard to the single-storey refrigerated structure you have rented from a woman called Joyce might as well be the yard of your homestead. A thousand thousand murders cleared the way for you to be here, enough blood to fill the bellies of every cannibal who ever lived, and not in the days of Job and Mordecai but in the days of your great-great-grandfather. Pour the caipirinhas. You will sleep with the raven-haired girl soon, under the air-con. Perhaps all four of you will go at each other, right here. It's not out of the question, and who would see, beyond the coyotes?

\ *lindsay* \

THEY WILL call you a veteran when you are ten-years-old. Your performance as two identical sisters will be described as soulful and adept, and the film will earn a hundred million dollars. Are there a hundred million stars when you look up, in your tenth year on the planet, little veteran? Draw a square and count. There just might be.

How about when you look up, age three? Three-year-old Ford Model, signed and contracted. Are there a hundred million bubbles in the soda as it spills? A hundred different colours in the photographer's eyes? A million O's in the bowl? Are there a hundred million hearts stuffed within your father's shirt, and if there are—how many of them love you?

The woman who plays your mother knows a thing or two—you're practically fully grown now, ripe for plucking, and she waltzes through that vineyard world of pluckers like she hasn't got two single fucks to give. She makes you laugh—she's a joker. The two of you switch bodies. Imagine—as you're studying her vocal patterns—how her body would really feel. Can you fill it up right to the corners, the tips? Split your consciousness and walk around in her tights for a bit. Feel the background chainsaw buzz ebb away to nothing. Isn't that nice. Does it remind you of being two? Can anything

217

remind you of being two? Can any portal transport you back to those days of comforters, before the photographers' eyes aimed themselves at you? No. You need another body for that.

It is hardly surprising, really, when the world decides that it's done with you. Perhaps the world has a maximum capacity for love. At some point, we are just too tired to be kind. At some point, we are sick to fucking death of you. At some point we require you to plunge head-first into your nosedive. At its terminus, we will finally be able to reassess you, perhaps even to love you again. To appreciate the things we once appreciated in you. To see the child we have ceased to be able to see. To stop masturbating to pictures of you. To stop taking pictures of you over your garden wall. To stop writing articles about your failings. To stop reading articles about your failings. To stop wanting to know about your failings. To stop enjoying your failings. To stop enjoying your losses. To stop enjoying your destruction. Because, at that point, your destruction will have finished. You will be, once more, small, big-eyed and adept, forever. And we can all appreciate that.

vi.

\ *that's that* \

THE BREAK that decides it comes out

of nowhere. She is twenty-six, and has just signed a book deal. She has cracked her lung jogging, shattered the casing around her gall bladder, but all had essentially been no biggie—bed rest and vitamin supplements had got her back on her feet. This one was different.

There's a shard lodged in your kidney, the doctor tells her. That's where the pain's been coming from. The pain had been unusually terrible, but she'd thought it might go away. You've been bleeding internally for weeks—I'm surprised you're still *con*scious. So, we'll need to open you up and take a look.

Neil calls several times, messages. WHERE are you? WHAT is up? Neil is a forceful messager. He is permanently message-furious. She doesn't want him around for this, so she tells him she's had to fly to New York for work. I'm actually going to meet Malcolm Gladwell, she says. Can u belieeev that? WOW, he message-yells, and then says nothing else.

She discharges herself whilst the doctor is on his rounds, buys a pack of the strongest non-prescription painkillers in Boots, and walks the street, hand pressed to abdomen like a hernia-sufferer. The pain is delirious, sacrilegious—she remembers Italian art films about Jesus, the wounds, the crown of thorns. She thinks: this is it. I am a glass bell, being chimed. I am an experiment going wrong. I am shanking myself to death, right now, as I walk down Berwick Street. What a ridiculously stupid and amazing way to pop your clogs. What a holy fucking farce. She could go back to hospital, get opened up, for the thousandth time, but what fun would that be? She understands that this is the end she was meant for, and she is ready to embrace it. She is the Glass Organs Girl. She finds a jazz bar. It is called: Jazz Bar. Backstreet Godardians clicking their fingers. It smells of bitters and Galoise. This is perfect, she thinks, entering the dim to the squelch of a winding-down sax routine. Several people glance her way: look—it's the Glass Organs Girl!

\ *all the people you've ever loved,*
or a process of unbecoming \

I RETURN to the production, headnude. The Writer is not on set. He got a commission in Berlin I think, a Mikkelsen tells me, but he had told me himself, in the folds of his duvet, in his little apartment in a tower block off Amagerbrogade. It's for a TV show, some drama in development. Immigration stories. Is quite good.

You'll be there a while, huh? Until after the end of the shoot? He nodded gently, eyes on his navel.

Have you visit Berlin?

They plaster me in. First, they enclose me in a skull cap. Then they baste me with adhesive gel. Glad to have you back, they say, thought you'd gotten away from us! The silicon slips over my head like a panic, sounds squashed. Putty is applied. There are brushes for fine detail. Glue on the eyelids, to smooth the join. The motherly make-up woman's voice comes from eternity. Her moist palms shift from the prosthetic to the parts of me that are me, and back, and the mirror presents a simple truth.

Does it? Are mirrors objective? Does it depend on the eyes? What use are eyes anyway, if all they show is a rough cut?

Berlin? No, never have. Munich once. I dawdled a finger on the sheets, next to his bruised hip. Gooseberry blue. He made us thick, strong coffee in little ceramic cups, painted with golden flowers, and we didn't bring it up again.

There was a boy, when I was still a child, a girl when I was less so. She handled me like chipped china. I wanted her to remind me of him.

There was another girl, a young woman I suppose — could we have been that, young man and woman? Surely not. She'd had a dagger run all up her insides, just carved her right open, and we licked each others' wounds for longer than anyone could say was healthy, until we were both less than we had been, and she took her turn to carve me.

There was a friend. I kissed his head once. I decided to keep him with me, always, by never showing him my heart.

There was a wife. Fuck me, what a shitshow.

And there was a man, a gentle man, with bruises on his hips and scripts to write. Sometimes, significance only lasts a few days. When that happens, you must let it go, like reeds in a stream passing over your submerged face. They're only reeds. Let them pass. They break so easily if you clutch. They're only reeds.

LET THEM GO! I scream, rubber-lipped. The thugs turn their attentions to me.

What da fuck is dis thing? one spits, terror and amusement on his toady mug, and he lowers the knife from the boy's throat. I smash the nearby pillar—semi-invisible cables yank it away. I hurl the iron-esque table—it splits soundlessly in two. I decide not to mutilate the surviving thug—I'm better than that. I carry the boy and his mother back across the bridge. We sit by the water, out behind the disused factory. It's magic hour, a reflector board bouncing the sunset onto the Danish-Algerian actress's chin. Who *are* you? she asks. I deliver the best work of my career. I unfold myself over myself, I peel myself in front of them all: the actress, the boy, the skeleton crew, the visiting co-producer. I let all of my sheaths come down. I step out of the second skin.

Cut, the director says. Wow. Wow man. Great. Really, really great. *Great* job. You got another one in you?

I nod my prosthetic. Sure.

I think we can do it maybe... twice? Twice more before the light goes. Okay with you?

Yeah. Whatever you need.

Awesome. Okay guys, reset.

The plane takes me above the clouds. The evening sun is sitting, pouring orange light like a blanket, dark at the rims. The kind of view that might make you invent a system of gods. London is damp. The basement flat is cold, and smells of shoes, and the rain—I've been away for weeks. I close each window, save for the kitchen. I leave a few inches, for the air to get in. I boil tea water. In the toaster's bent reflection, my head is my own, more or less. The window shows a slice of ground level, passing feet. Down the wall, from the upstairs doorway: a spillage of hydrangeas.

THEY WANT it fresh, on-point,

and three jokes every page. Everything else, you got freedom. Fresh, on-point, three jokes a page.

What does fresh mean?

Jesus Joey, you gonna ride me on this?

What does on-point mean?

You gonna ride my ass? Really? Really. You're gonna my ass on this.

He's grouchy because I'm right. He takes a sulky sip of his spirulina dacquiri.

The guy's a fucking moron Zach. He doesn't know how to write a *knock*-knock joke.

Well then it's a good thing they've hired *you*, and that I okayed an *incredibly* generous salary. You're welcome.

He just charges around the stage like a retard off his ritalin. He's like a rung below Dane *Cook*.

That's. Why. They've— Jesus, I am *not* having this con— take the fucking job or *don't* take the fucking job Joey, but *stop*. *Riding. My. Ass.*

He's like Napoleon Dynamite's less cool fake-jock cousin.

Joey—

He's like Emilio Estevez in Breakfast Club after he hits

that joint and turns into the Energizer Bunny, only instead of Emilio Estevez he's Emilio Estevez's retarded cousin Brent.

That's two cousins Joey, you're repeating yourself. Check please? Now?

He's like—

I will stab you Joey, you wanna be stabbed?

I have WGA health insurance, just aim away from the vital organs.

The Idiot sits there, in his beachwear, looking at me like a dog that's been shown a card trick.

I dunno dude, I mean—he adjusts his thighs—I always hated those shows that feel overwritten, you know? Like when it's all like, like you can see every, like, machination of the plot?

Right. But you do *need* a plot, so—

I like the Seinfeld thing—a show about nothing! Let's do one of those.

I would like to remove his orange-lensed aviators and insert them about his person.

Right, but Seinfeld actually has some of the tightest plotting in situation comedy—

It's a show about nothing!

Inserted rectally, sideways, or perhaps down his oesophegus, or hell maybe the former and then the latter.

Well, we *need* an A plot with a *protag*onist, a B plot with a *protag*onist—

God, chillax Josephine! W'ell get it man, we'll get it. I'm

just telling you what I like. And I'm pretty sure it's your job to put what I like on the page, feel me?

He takes us on a ride to Hermosa Beach, to 'bond'. I would rather bond my ass to someone else's ass. That's the thing about this town man, he's saying, literally driving one-handed, left arm literally resting on the open window, in his literal 2017 blood red Honda convertible. It's like... it's like it's all fraud man! The whole thing! Every motherfucker's just showing their fake selves, hoping to catch the worm, you know? I don't wanna do that.

What worm?

Money worm, motherfucker.

I've known his type before, all my life: the cocky little cat that got the cream. Spoojing over girlie girls in high school, knuckling math club skulls—no, no, not alpha jock, no, more damaged over-compensator: daddy left his mommy and almost never called, so he studied lacrosse technique and lead guitar and grew his hair out and finger-fucked codependents out back of the local rec centre, and got into coke and business school, until he dropped out to be an 'actor'. Stand-up comedy fall-back. Doing prop routines, goofball shit. He pulls up by a bandstand on a cliff overlooking the ocean. You know what that is? Come on.

He leads us to the bandstand. The echo of each step has seven echoes. So you gonna sing, or—?

This is the spot where I got sober. He closes his eyes, takes a lungful of air. Aaah. Yeah, brother. Right here. He takes something like a poker chip from his pocket, flicks it to me. That's my eight year chip. Got it yesterday. I turn it over. To Thine Own Self Be True. A triangle with an embossed 8. I slip it in my pocket.

Dude, he says.

Don't worry, you'll get it back if you're good.

He gives me the lizard look: sizing up its prey.

We gotta work together dude. I'm the man, you're the man's right hand. You got a problem being my right hand?

I dunno, which hand do you wipe your ass with?

He genuinely laughs, puts a heavy arm around me. I can feel the damp heat of his pit. Come on man, put the shields down. Opposites attract. We're gonna be a fuckin awesome team. Okay. Alright? I allow him the nod he's looking for. Alright. He holds out a hand. Chip.

Little do you know, CoDA finger-fucker. Little do you know.

Joey!

Heeey, Zachariah Zeffeniah. You're out in the hours of daylight. What gives? Appointment at the STD clinic?

Where the hell is Jimmie?

I'll take that as a yes. Hey careful man, I think if your kind cross the threshold to a writers' room without an invitation you turn to dust, right?

Joseph!

Relax. Haven't seen him. But he's been taking the whole process pretty hard, and, well, you know he's sober right? I

230

mean, was sober. I think—

Are you shitting me? Are you shitting in my ass right now?

If wishing made it so, Babooshka.

We're delivering a pilot script *and* a show bible in a week!

As the head writer, I have been impressing that point upon—

Where is he!

Yeah, honestly, much as I love this job you got me, I've got better things to be doing that chasing around alcoholic shitheels and playing crisis counsellor, and I actually have a couple of offers—

Oh you do huh? Who?

Mel, and Scott—both got development deals, putting rooms together. I mean not to be a quitter, but I think once you track down the idiot-sans-savant you'll agree that it's time to pack this carnival up for the season, cash our cheques and move on to the next town, capiche?

Oh that right huh?

That's just the way it is, friendo. Wadn't my idea to give him a show.

Uh huh, right. Think again, friendo.

Zachary, baby, if you think I'm impressed by the Don Draper routine—

You've got a six-month non-compete clause. Check your contract. You don't have to work on this show, but you won't be working anywhere else for half a year. Oh, not so fast with the quippage now? Find him, chain him to that god-damn chair, and get me a functioning script by Friday or, I *swear* to *God* Joe, every producer in town is gonna know who botched this, and it ain't gonna be me, friendo.

The motel room smells like a dead man's groin. It hits you in the face like a flannel. Jee sus Christ man. How long you been in here? Seriously, have you been shitting in the wastepaper basket or something?

I can't... I can't do it.

He's crouched on the bed, in boxer briefs and a filthy Mighty Ducks t-shirt, rocking, feet pressing deep indentations into the mattress.

Oh for God's sake.

I move a pair of jeans and a bottle of Johnnie Walker from a chair with thumb-and-forefingers, sit. I feel like I'm gonna get tetanus just breathing in here.

You were right, he says. You were right man. He flicks his tongue around his mouth, cat-like, so dry and sticky I can hear it.

Well, I usually am.

No—he leans his head forward, thinks about standing, decides against. You were right! What the fuck am I man? Who the fuck *am* I? To have... to have a *show*?

Jesus! I was *fuck*ing with you! God, you're-- you're *the* Jimmie Di Santo! Right? Right?

He's staring at some shitty reproduction of an impressionist bleurgh hanging on the wall by the bedside table. What do you think that means?

That painting? It means that Frenchmen have too much time on their hands.

232

He tilts his head. It looks like... like a pool.

It's abstract, genius.

Like a red and yellow pool...

Hey! Jimmie. Alright. Enough. All that shit I said, totally not true. You're the man, I'm a bitter asshole, okay? That what you wanted to hear? I was *fuck*ing with you to *test* you, to see if you could handle your shit in this business, okay? Eeeeveryone does it, it's like traditional or whatever.

A haze... he says, still tilted.

Right, like in college, only wittier. So, long story short: erase all I said. It was all part of the haze. And you passed. Flying colours.

You... you said I didn't have a— what... a TV—

Personality, yes, I did, and I really—

You said there was no point writing up the plotlines—

Because you had no understanding of causality, I did—

You said—

I said a lot, I know—

You told the other writers not to turn in ideas—

Because you had to learn, yes—waaay too harsh, I see that now, *but*, Jimmie, dude, it's *good* because... because *now*, shard ordeal man! Bonding. Now we're in the trenches together. Okay? Now I'm on board.

You weren't on-board before.

No I was not, I admit it.

You didn't want it to work.

Hey—there's a fine line between paranoia and—

Admit it. You didn't.

Okay. Alright. I didn't. I didn't think you deserved it. But I am one trillion percent on-board now.

Because you have to be. Right?

Well— I—

Because Zach told you about the non-compete clause?

I—

Yeah, you don't have one of those.

He hops off the bed, stretches his back, picks up the half-full bottle of Johnnie and glug glug glugs, tosses it into my lap.

Aaaaah. But — he picks up his cellphone form the dresser, shows me the screen: a microphone icon, waveform – I have a feeling it's not gonna make much diff. Think you're out of a job, friendo.

As he pulls his pants on, and calls Zach, I take a glug of what seems to be apple juice.

Oh—he says, taking the phone away from his mouth—I think you still have my chip? You can keep that. Little memento. Hey, if you tell people it's Jimmie Di Santo's maybe you can get something for it. Could come in handy, 'cause I don't think you're gonna be getting this month's paycheque.

If you could write a message on the sky, you would, and it would say

When you, world, finally see me for what I am, you, world, will get down on your knees and...

You're *dropping* me? The hell do you mean? You're *dropping* me?

Past tense Joe, as in -ed ending: dropped.

The hell does that even *mean*?

Five jobs in a row. Complaints, complaints, complaints—
I've got *my* reputation to think about. And I talked to Zach,
so don't even—

Fine, you''re small time anyway.

Ha ha... yeah. Good luck Joe, you're gonna need it.

You're fuckin small time, your contacts suck—

Joan? Have security escort Joe—

HA! Fuck you security!

Oh, *please* put up a struggle Joe, I'll get the popcorn.

Seven years of screen credits, I've got my own series in
development—

With who?

It was with Bright Star, now we're looking—

So it's not in development anymore?

No, it is, we're looking—

Who's we?

Me, my team—

So, you?

And my team—

Yeah, see, Joe, we've heard about you and the Jimmie
Show fiasco, everyone has, and frankly no-one is surprised.
So I don't think you'll be getting a lot of joy right—

But it's bullshit! *Seven* years—

G'bye Joe.

SEVEN years—

When you look in the mirror, what do you see? What do you see looking back at you? It's not you, right? Not exactly. You don't exist in that thing. That thing's all backwards, for a start. I don't know, I'm rambling. But seriously, what *do* you see? Me—I'm a writer. Screen, mostly—comedy, some drama. It's like, the characters you create—you're their god. And what are they, when they're on a screen, talking to each other, fighting, fucking each other—they're not me, and yet they *are* me. It's—are you following me?

Joe! Table seven's been waiting a half hour, the hell are you—

Alright, alright, I'm on it, Jesus.

Fucking thirty-year-old man, I have to get on your ass to do your job?

I said I'm on it Ernesto!

On it too fuckin slow, Joseph! Pick up your game or get back to the out-of-work wannabe screenwriters' welfare line, bitch.

What did you say to me?

I said, pick your—aaaaah!

Say it again, Ernesto!

Julio! Agarra a ese cabron!

Get offa me! Bitch ass bitch! Get— mgm— off!

Gimme the ladle, moron!

Because, when you think about it, who *is* God? I mean, the Christian God? Am I right? Pfff, I mean— human form, white dude in beard? Some asshole's feel-better father fantasy,

236

right? Like, like a...

Panacea?

Right. Like a panacea. Cure-all ills. Bull! And don't get me started on the Indian shit, a *thousand* of the fuckers, and the arms and shit—

If you're talking Hinduism, it's thirty-three million.

What!

Thirty-three million gods.

Thirty-three... how many people even are there for— what, a hundred million Hindus, maximum?

A billion.

A billion Hindus? Pfff. I can't even... that's like—

A god for every thirty people.

Right! Bullshit!

Sounds nice to me. You and the other twenty-nine can get together every week and discuss your god's performance. Like a job review. Tell me that's not attractive.

Pfff... it's bullshit anyway. You know what godliness is, know what a fuckin deity is?

A drunk thirty-year-old in skater jeans?

Yo. Di Santo.

He pauses, hand on the open car door, leaking car-cool air.

Jesus dude. The hell happened to you man?

I realised my inner godliness.

The bottle doesn't smash on his head—thick dull thud, too much still in there, but down he goes, and it's better, because no glass to clear up and still liquor to drink.

You know if you look up at the sun you see pools of light, yellow and red?

Yeah. So?

Look for too long – more than a second or two even – you'll fry your retinas. Burned like french fries stuck to the side of the fryer.

Pfff, you gonna give me the Mexican, Indian, the sun is our god baloney? Danny Boyle tried that shit man, turned out the monster did it.

You probably think it's damage, right? The beginnings of the burn? That's the pool, right?

I dunno man. Sure.

But it's not.

...Who are you again?

Tying him to the seat is harder than you think—the twine is fiddly, scissors not sharp enough, have to hack and saw, and he's only out cold for a minute, tops, then it's the groggy come-around, the groaning, so on with the gag—Crips style head flag and a strip of duct tape, chin dimple to filtrum.

Beautiful drive, huh? I say, once we're off the freeway. Awesome thing is, if you had regular windows and not these tinted gangsta things we'd've got like twenty feet before someone called the cops. So thanks.

His eyes bely the fear. Anxious little bunny. It fills me up like springtime.

Who am I? Who are you? Are you a god, Joe?

Maybe I fuckin am.

Joseph James Simon McArthur, angry god of Indiana by way of Highland Park.

You're weirding me out now.

That's what I do my child. But you haven't asked. The pool—not burn damage. The sun—not god. What is it? The light?

What is the light?

That's what you have to ask.

Okay. What is the light?

Photobleaching. Visual perception.

Come again?

You see too much of one colour—holy nuclear cyan-white in this case—your photoreceptors play a trick. You're flooded with glimmering opposite. Pools of yellow and red. That's all it is. A trick of the light. A trick of the eyes. Nothing more to it than that.

But stare too long, you still get fried, right?

Most certainly.

I pull up by the bandstand, ocean crepuscular. Here we are, motherfucker. The place Jimmie Di Santo got sober. Ever occur to you you might've been funnier drunk?

He's eyeing me now, like he can see something about me. Oh hey, I still got your chip. I toss it into his lap, pour the liquor all over like a Christening. Smell good? Mmm, bourbon. Delish, right? Tell you what Jimmie, *the* Jimmie Di Santo, I'm'a leave this thing in drive. I snip two of the cords—

his right hand gaining freedom. Whoa there grabby! You got just enough reach to flip the handbrake, this thing'll rooooll all the way down to the edge there. Nice way to go, right? Or, you can sit here until someone decides to come take a look, if they can even see you from the road—two days? Three? Four? The ants'll be halfway through your nutsack by then, but who cares right? Oh, and you can explain—I reach into my backpack—the unlicensed revolver and bag of coke in the glovebox.

I let them hang in the air in front of him a moment, just so he can see they're real. His eyes go cartoon.

And you know what I'm gonna be doing, while you weigh up this dilemma? Pitching the Joe McArthur show, to platforms who know talent when they see it. Nighty night, you fucking hack.

Know how I know all this? Think I'm just a man in a bar?

You don't know all that much.

Joseph. Come on now. Take my hand. Yes, like that, let me lead you. Yes. Now. Look at yourself in the mirror. What do you see? Do you see a man? A boy? A god? An empty shell? A little piece of each and every one? Do you see your past? Can you see your future? The world will try to tell you you're like everybody else. But you're not like everybody else, are you? You see that chasm within? No, don't look into it! Look above it. You're free now. You're a creator of lives. A bringer of worlds. You're a magic maker, a spirit diviner. You bring silence to chattering minds, comfort to the uncomfortable. How like a god you are! Thirty-three million, and they're all better than you? Just because you're mistreated doesn't mean— how can I put this? The lion does not concern itself—

—with the opinions of the sheep. Game of Thrones. I love that scene.

Exactly. Come to my arms. Let me hold you. You know I was never here, right?

Of course. This is nice. Mm. What next?

I'm carving the date into my forearm, but keep getting stuck on the three. Next door's doorbell could be mine, but sirens could be distant too. I realise, too late, the need for disciples.

\jazz bar\

SHE FINDS a jazz bar. It is called: Jazz Bar. Inside, backstreet Godardians, Gauloise. She smooths the see-through raincoat. Eyes turn her way: it's the Glass Organs Girl!

Only—is it? Is that what she is? She remembers her taste for war films, the advice of the effective soldier: to accept that you are already dead. The ineffective soldier tried to accept this, volunteered for a dangerous mission, scouting a farmhouse, but he was faking—he hadn't really accepted that he was already dead, and that's why he was immediately shot in the neck. No fakers. Death punishes false prophets. Is she a prophet? Of a sort? If only to herself? The shard of her body's making, it's jagging at her kidney matter, she can feel it in there, underneath the numbness. She switches off that part of her body. It's surprisingly easy to do. Her breathing is shallow, like a bird's—if she had wings they would be a-flutter. A drum cascade crescendos. Men are sitting, men are dancing, a few women too. She is shanking herself to death, a holy fucking farce, and she understands she must dance, so she does. She twirls, the hem of her see-through raincoat spinning. A beardo applauds, the perv. So? Let them perv. Let them get their juices up as she spins into liquefaction. Let the fuckers spooj as she expires. Serve 'em right, wouldn't it? She ignores what may be nausea. Let's call it an empty stomach.

A waitress hands her a highball full of something gin-ish, points to a dim corner, where a glowing woman is watching her. The glowing woman nods. Her fella, a stubbly rumplo in a shoulder bag, seems to be in a world of his own. Sod it then, bottoms up? The lemon touches her teeth, and she travels back in time. She is fourteen, on a bench in the play area behind a leisure centre, glugging on a bottle of Sol, choking down the stale beer, but something's in the way — stuck in the neck, lemon wedge. Trackie Bottoms laughs at her, Skater Boy pelvis-thrusts the air. She is eleven, and the grass is summer long, the evening coming, her friend lying next to her talking about stars. You can see them, in the rosemilk sky, little diamantes, like on her friend's nails, sparkle sparkling more or less, and the rims dim, and her friend's fingers are touching lightly the pale hairs of her forearm, white chocolate on her teeth. And she is twenty, on a halls of residence single bed in Bremen being gentlefucked by Henning, his hand on the handles of her hips and his exhalations coming Danish, glottal, soft, she is in her flat with Lucy watching The Elephant Man, seeing her life represented in John Merrick's and trying to hide from Lucy's increasingly unsympathetic eyes the tears. She is running hand-in-hand with a pretty tomboy through the tents of a music festival, in a summer flush and tripping balls on mushroom tea, and the tents are filling with all the moments of her life: long-forgotten quiet moments with people she'd abandoned, childhood Christmases, father-daughter snowfights, sexual misadventures, whole day hangovers. The glowing woman is coming for her. She's saying something, the glowing woman. It's hard to account for the glow, but it's there. She's saying something about a secret, a key. She's saying something about the universe. She's dancing next to her, hands over head and fringe-flicking.

What the fuck do you want?

But the jazz blots out her words. She downs another gin-ish thing. She is thirteen, syphoning Bombay Sapphire into a plastic milk bottle, mixing it with Sainsbury's Tropical. The glowing woman has disappeared, but a hand touches her arm and red-yellow pools of light fill her vision. Red-yellow pools—like as if you' were a kid and looked too long at the sun. Red-yellow pools of light.

What does that mean exactly? asks the Actress.

I mean, it's up to you really. To your interpretation.

They are in the actual building—the actual Jazz Bar. It is no longer called Jazz Bar, but for the shoot, it has reverted. Veracity is important. It feels so to her, and so it is. She has learned there is no difference between what feels important to her and what is important. She does not know why she never realised this before.

Okay. I mean... okay. Okay, I get it. The Actress has a serious look. She is taking it seriously, the job of being her. Her British accent is very convincing. Well, you know, my ex-husband, she'd said with a shrug. It filters through. You shoulda heard me do it before. Good evenin' Guv'nor! She is looking at her sides, her lines highlighted, studying the words.

So, like... like why did you *do* this?

Beyond the actress, the female director is conversing with the grip team. A light is being adjusted. There is a real band on the stage, but the stage isn't where it used to be.

Why did I—?

Like—yeah. Why did you come here, instead of going to the hospital? Weren't you scared?

She considers this for a moment, but she is distracted. The speckles on the director's back, revealed by her vest-top, astride the horse-brown plait of her hair, remind her of white chocolate.

She goes with the Actress to all the bars. They Soho up a storm. Soho is not a scary place anymore, and she no longer has to pretend a thing. She is no longer the Glass Organs Girl. They talk LA, movies, paparazzi, ratfuck twats. They look at each other, examining their differences. Your forehead is prettier than mine, she tells the Actress, and the Actress does a head-back laugh that seems to be for real. Why thaaaaank you dahling. She strokes the Actress's face, in the Uber. It's a nice face, she says. The Actress is eyes-closed smiling. A nice face they chose for me. Lucky they could afford me, she guffaws. The Former Glass Organs Girl agrees. Yeah, she says, still stroking, it is lucky. She thinks, I'm gonna kiss her when we get back to mine, and maybe we'll undress each other, press our bodies together. Hers will be taughter and tanned, core-strong. The lines of her will be better than the lines of me. But my lines will be fine. My lines will be slim, only charmingly skewed. We will explore each other, see what happens when the expensive American me and the me me press against each other. Maybe, she thinks, half-aware of the Persion Uber driver politely keeping his eyes on the road, and the flutter of the Actress's still closed pretty eyes, maybe we'll see stars.

iiv.

THE FORMER Stuntman and the

no-longer teenage Actress fall in love. It is as stupid and as simple as that. There is no other way of looking at it, no ulterior motives; they simply fall in love. It is so simple he doesn't quite think it is happening.

They run around town. They sleep-in at her place, listen to her psychotic roommate chanting along to motivational videos as she blends avocados. They get high under an old boardwalk down near Hermosa Beach in the middle of a Tuesday afternoon, sunlight glimmering on the water. You're not like you look you know, she says, hash smoke hanging in the air like incense in a church.

How'd you mean? He hears his British accent floating back for a moment.

Look at you! she says, squeezing his arm. You're like a *meat*head. But you're not, and she nuzzles into his shoulder. He looks at her as they walk, at how the breeze catches her bangs. She is very beautiful, he thinks, but not in the way everyone else thinks she is. *I'm* the one who knows why she's beautiful, he thinks, and he wonders for a moment if this is problematic, possessive. No, he thinks, no it's probably okay.

His place is a loft apartment in Culver City, that he shares with an Egyptian guy who's never home. A dark little driveway bordered by overhanging shrubs. They sit in his Toyota, in the driveway, the engine idling, returned from the beach, listening to a song they like playing out on the radio, nuzzling, talking, enjoying the end of the trip before they have to go inside. Then another good one comes on and they let that one play through too.

I don't practice santeria
I ain't got no crystal ball
Well I had a million dollars, but I—
I spent it all

So what did you, like... she says, and the flickering light from Mrs Jimenez's porch is flickering in her eyes, ...like... like what did you think life would be like? Did you think it'd be like this?

Pff. No. No, not at all.

When you were in *Eng*land—she screws up her mouth and makes her SNL voice.

Ha, no. No, I never really... I was just some skinny kid from Milton Keynes, I never... I just came out here to try and work.

And now you're a *movie star*! She jazz hands, makes her eyes big. He likes her performances. She makes jokes where there were no jokes. She makes fun where there would otherwise be emptiness.

Well. What—grand total of about nineteen lines? Don't think I'm Ryan Gosling yet.

Fuck that guy.

When they make their way up the exterior stairs there's a stereo playing in the distance, the smell of lavender in the air from Mrs Jimenez's patio garden. His place is cool—he'd left the windows open—and quiet, and dark. They go to sleep next to each other, and he feels no self-consciousness at all. He looks at her when he wakes. She has her teenhood etched in her face, he thinks, her bizarre and tumultuous teenhood, it's all in there. That's why she is beautiful. She mutters something in her sleep. He strokes the hair away from her cheek. She murmurs and shifts into him. He hears Sayid returning.

XIANG Xiaotong watches the actor. He knows the Actor was not always an actor. For many years, the Actor was a stuntman — paid to be kicked in the chest, hurled through the air. Xiang Xiaotong does not respect these stuntmen. They are, in his experience, inadequate morons. He himself has sent hundreds of them flying backwards through exploding walls and plates of sugar glass. But he is not a terrible actor this one, and his British accent suits the role. The role which, in the original, was Xiang Xiaotong's. Which, unmistakably and indissolubly, will always be Xiang Xiaotong's, no matter how the American moneybrains recast.

The way Xiang Xiaotong played the character (a government penpusher whose wife and child are slaughtered, who loses ninety percent of his sight and has to learn from a master to fight blind if he is to avenge his family), with a Yunnan accent and bumpkin mannerisms, he was always an outsider, and audiences gulped him up, begged for sequels, which doubled and tripled the takings of the original. But this is America, and they want their heroes Western. The producers made sure he was cast as the Master, a sign of 'respect'. You are this franchise, they'd said, in the meeting room in Culver City, over a platter of sugar-encrusted dough. We gotta have Xiang

Xiaotong in there. They'd butchered his name of course.

But he is not the Master. He is the Outsider. He knows this. Everyone knows this. He has accepted their offer, and the phenomenal paycheque—this is simple pragmatism. But he knows who he is.

He watches the Actor, eyeballing a private-hire mercenary, unflinching, as the mercenary soft-talks. The lights are thrumming, bright as novas, and machine smoke hangs at shin level. He doesn't know how the audience can be expected to understand a word of this mumbling nonsense, but fine—this is America. The Actor's face shifts, and a henchman's brow drips sweat: a double-cross is coming. As the bell rings, the former stuntman grins at Xiang Xiaotong, wiping his face with a towel and heading over, the crew milling around him.

What have think you? he says, in his beginner's Cantonese. He has made the effort, Xiang Xiaotong thinks, and this at least is commendable. It's not his fault he sounds like a halfwit. It puts him three-eighths of wit ahead of the fucking Americans.

Their upcoming scene is a turning point. They are by the waterfall, and the Outsider's resolve has broken. Sick of lugging water pails on his back up and down the mountain, he has fallen to the ground, and seeing the military issue combat knife poking from his backpack he discovers his intention— he will kill the Master.

Ah, says the Master.

The Outsider looks up from the ground. He hadn't heard

him approach. The Master is balanced on one leg on one of the waterfall's ledges, tumult flowing around him.

You wish to end your suffering, the Master says, eye muscles tensing.

The Outsider squares his jaw.

Of course! Because you are a worm. Okay worm, and he slow-leaps three run-off channels to land within striking distance. Do as the cowardly worm does. But remember—

He fans himself, stretches a hand.

—I am the crane.

I'm thinking I should be on my knees here, the Actor says. Xiang Xiaotong is uncomfortable being in the Actor's trailer. It smells of lotion.

You know, on my knees? Like this.

The Actor drops to his knees. Xiang Xiaotong looks at him.

Like, it's a bit more... I dunno, I like the symbolism better? What do you think? The Actor's pectorals detense in his too-tight t-shirt.

Xiang Xiaotong tells the translator that if the Outsider were on his knees, the Master would decapitate him, and that if he wants to choreograph their fight scenes he is welcome to try. He looks out of the window as the translator struggles to rephrase his comment. The Belgian Pop Star is out there, talking with one of her girl-servants.

The Actor is nodding. Yeah, yeah, yeah. Well let's run through it with me on my knees? And then compare? Okay?

Xiang Xiaotong adds 'punish translator' to his mental list

of chores. The Belgian Pop Star is not listening to her girl-servant. The Belgian Pop Star is gazing through the window at the Actor.

He has been watching them since he arrived. She, with her underlobe tattoos, her blonde streaks, her deliberately emphasised beauty mole, her retinue of servants (mostly girls, some homosexuals). She is not even beautiful. She thinks she is, but she is not. Zhang Ziyi is beautiful. She is a toad in princess garb. He told the translator to tell her this, and watched the evolution of expressions for several seconds before dismissing him. The Belgian Pop Star, of course, believes that because he is Chinese he is somewhere near the level, status-wise, of a 5-year-old or a well-behaved Alsatian. When she mouth-smiles at him, he encourages her to go and drink her own toilet water. She nods and smiles back. Sometimes she adds a hair-flick. His favourite is when she adds the hair-flick. He estimates that she has been fellating the Actor since the second week of rehearsals.

How is the director? the image of his wife's face asks. She appears to be applying nail varnish out-of-shot.

An imbecile, of course. They're all imbeciles.

Not all? she says, attention diverted.

Close enough.

She is not listening to him, again. Beyond her, he can hear her assistants organising a photo-shoot. There are model girls and model boys around her, somewhere, having their cheekbones painted, their lashes coated, their chests moisture dappled, gossiping their gossip, dispensing their hubris. She tells a nearby assistant, gentle-voiced, to replenish her coffee. The assistant calls her Madam Zhi-Zhi. They all call her Madam Zhi-Zhi. She doesn't have to ask them to—they want to call her Madam Zhi-Zhi. She asks what scene they're shooting today.

You can call me later, when you can spare more of your valuable attention, he says.

She baby-poos her brow and nostril-huffs. Big Treasure, I'm listenin—

Goodbye!

He remembers, as her contorted image hangs, frozen, on the surface of the tablet, their early days—how obedient she'd been, how attentive. He should have known better.

He watches the Belgian Pop Star as she line-reads with one of her retinue. She has a faint cluster of downy hairs around the ball of her jaw, like a sixteen-year-old girl, and she is performing a scene of pre-confrontation tension when she catches sight of the Actor passing on his cellphone. A coquettish warmth wipes over her face. She winks—her servant play-slaps her shoulder. The Actor is talking to his wife, consoling—Xiang Xiaotong hears something about escape.

So if I'm failing, teach me! roars the imposter Outsider. He has collapsed into the marshland under the weight of his stone-filled pack.

The Master (who is really the Outsider) elevates himself, a full inch taller.

What you lack cannot be taught, he says. You are weak. You are disciplineless. You are a do-nothing. Why don't you do what you wish to do, and let the marsh engulf you. He fans his arms like wings, and the waters rise, the mud shifts, the wind levels up, the very earth begins to suck the imposter Outsider down into the muck.

What's happening? I can't-- I can't— help!

But the Master (who is really the Outsider) has closed his eyes, tilted up his chin, and he is rising along with the waters, ballerina-toed and balanced on the surface like an angel of death.

It is the end of a seventeen-hour shoot day. Slovenly grips, sweat-sheened, have switched to beer, leaning on equipment vans, grousing, guffawing, and the exhausted director is in discussion with two jeaned producers. They are looking at Xiang Xiaotong. They are talking to the translator. They are approaching. Ah... I'm sorry—

The translator is nodding, listening to the producers. One smiles a stubbly smile. His crow's feet have crow's feet.

Ah, sorry— the honourable producers are very sorry, but... yes, there is some problem with the scene, and they wish to ask if you would be willing to do one more or two more takes, because--

It's midnight, says Xiang Xiaotong.

Yes — the translator nervous laughs — the honorable producers say only one or two hours more, at the maximum limit, because there is no time in the schedule later--

Tell them they have the eyes of lizards.

Ah—

Common lizards. Tell them.

Ah— honorable sir, the honorable producers express their discomfort at asking this of you, but they assure me your contract stipulates—

The Actor is on the set, doing push-ups.

Xiang Xiaotong makes a gesture which the translator understands full well.

TEACH ME! roars the imposter Outsider. He has changed: he is full of heart now, full of fire. For a moment, Xiang Xiaotong is thrown. He elevates himself.

What you lack cannot be taught. He feels the power in his voice. It radiates through him. A darkness washes over the set. He tells the imposter Outsider he is weak. He tells him he is disciplineless. The imposter Outsider, broken, on his hands in the mud, is full now of terrible shards. The Master-Outsider raises his hands, and the marsh rises. He raises himself (he cannot feel the wires now—they have become like ribs) and watches as the imposter Outsider sinks. He roars for help, a piteous animal, full of pain and fury. It is very close to convincing.

Xiang Xiaotong refuses the drinks—he will not drink with

these men. He watches them, smiles at the right points, gives a laugh. It is gone 2am, and elation has bonded them, these men. The work man! It's all about moments like this! When you know you're photographing pure moving gold? How fucken often does that shit happen, really? Xiang Xiaotong agrees that rare are such moments. He feels, suddenly, extremely tired. He wishes his wife were here. He would forgive her her ills, and she would stroke his head, hold him to her slender breast. He would ask for the news of their son, if he had called. The Actor, too, looks suddenly exhausted. He is on his phone again, to his wife, pleading, consoling. The Belgian Pop Star has not left the set—her car is still outside her trailer, and through one of the trailer's windows he can see the faint glow of a tinted lamp.

He finds himself thinking of his father. Of his tempers, the bleak tides that would wash over him and sweep him away, how he'd return with the snake in his eyes, the reprimands, the lashes, the angry red welts. A sudden, unbidden thought emerges: that he has remade the old man. A moon of truths eclipses his red dwarf heart. Quickly, he smothers it with clouds. He joins the producers in their bourbon. It is cold on the set, so late, or early, whichever. Someone places a coat around his shoulders. When I was a lad, he tells the men, via the translator, I was a genius. You haven't seen my early work, no-one here has, but I was incredible. So strong. I did a thousand pull-ups every morning—a thousand! Like it was nothing! No no, I've seen 'em! I've seen 'em! the director is saying. Coil of the Serpent? Man, I love you in that, it's amayzing! And Red Spring? Are you kidding me? The halberd scene? The translator is reporting the director's breathless praise, himself beaming, and the producers are laughing and clapping him on the back. He isn't aware that he is about to cry until it is too late.

He is leaning his head on the plush, scented leather headrest in the back of the car, the driver pulling away from the set, and all the feelings there. The digital clock says 3:11am, and the car's interior is soothing—a gentle burble from the radio, the glow of the dashlights. The radio says something about a suicide—a Danish director, festival darling. Set for big things, in town for meetings, found in his hotel room with a self-inflicted bullet wound. Xiang Xiaotong has never heard of him. The car slows to a halt. He asks the African American driver what he's doing. I dunno, somethin's goin' on, he says, distracted, lowering his window. Y'all got a flat?

As the Belgian Pop Star nestles into the comfortable leather beside him, Xiang Xiaotong assesses her. As she proffers tired pleasantries. There is the faintest pale scar along the rim of her filtrum, and, head leant back, a pleasant doughy musculature to her neck. He decides that she is somewhat beautiful after all. He remembers a willowy Taiwanese composer from one of his earliest features, a weekend in Kowloon Bay. A half-French actress-poet who'd come close to denouncing her wealth for him, and would have, if he'd been willing to denounce his wife. About the film he'd made with a certain beautiful superstar—perhaps the only woman who'd ever managed to make a boy of him. About the hospital waiting room in Dongzhimen, where he'd eaten strips of pomelo and smoked as his only son emerged, a corridor away, from the loins of his wife. About the traces of matter from his wife's womb that remained on the babe's miniature forehead as the nurse placed the child, wriggling and light as origami, into his arms. The Belgian Pop Star has receded into the glow of her cellphone. Strip malls and darkness beyond the windows' tint. In tomorrow's scene, the Actor will defeat him. Xiang Xiaotong watches the passing darkness.

\ *ruan lingyu* \

A SPRAY of Plum Blossoms. The Goddess. She answers an ad, fifteen-year-old daughter of a house-servant, fifteen-year-old daughter of the republican era, daughter of the Three Principles of the People. The Qing dynasty had crumbled when she was barely a year, as if she'd heralded the collapse herself. She answers an ad, fifteen-year-old girl, skinny servant's daughter, from the Mingxing Film Company. A year later and she's on the screen: A Married Couple In Name Only. She is effervescent, they say, impressively elegant, they say—sixteen-year-old daughter of a house-servant widow and a decade-dead father, unskilled worker, from Asiatic Petroleum, in the afterlife now throwing mah jong with her other ancestors. Fatherless from six. We lose the ones we love. We lose the ones who love us. Sometimes, all we have is our elegance.

She is a daughter of Sun Yat-sen's new era, a starling of the republican dawn. Her eyes are elongated opals, overspilling hurts. Sometimes, to the dark rooms of workers in Shanghai, Guangzhou, Beijing, Chengdu, it will seem as if she is emerging through the screen, her image twenty-feet tall and glittering grey, and if you know her story you will see her dead father and her servant mother just under her two-storey surface, as the camera presses in.   Women will find their breath has caught, men will stir at the shift of her dress, sixteen, seventeen, eighteen-year-old daughter of the servant widow. The fourth son of the family her mother serves will take Ruan to court, claiming that she is his wife, and a thief. Her new partner, Tang, the tycoon, will already be engaged in an affair with another actress. The fourth son, a gambler, will launch a second lawsuit, accusing Ruan of adultery. It is the third decade of Sun Yat-sen's new era. The newspapers know a good story when they see one. They fill their pages with the fallen Goddess. Margin to margin, on factory floors in Tianjin, tea shops in Wuhan, libraries in Beijing, street stalls and markets in Yunnan and Hunan, thief, adulterer, whore, harlot, fraud, servant, pleb, slut, cheat, fraud, thief, liar, witch, golddigger, harpee, dog. Her films continue to play, rescreened in the cities, the provinces. In New Women, she plays an actress destroyed by circumstance. In A Spray of Plum Blossoms, true love somehow evades her.

Her suicide note reads:

gossip is a fearful thing

The procession for the funeral, Ruan's funeral, twenty-five-year-old Ruan, skinny effervescing Ruan, sixteen-year-old Couple In Name Only Ruan, six-year-old daughter of ghosts Ruan, is three miles long. As the cart bearing her small body is pulled, by six horses, through the crowds, numbering in the tens of thousands, three other women take their lives. Three daughters, wives, who cannot bear the young Goddess's absence. Three daughters who understand shame, caprice, and roomfuls of men. They take their lives. Take? They end their lives. They die, right there, in the crowd, with Ruan, as if to say: me too.

She will be played by Maggie Cheung, sixty years later, and Maggie Cheung will win Best Actress at Berlin. Her name will not appear in Western histories of the silent era, daughter of the Three Principles, who effervesced, a teenager. To look at her, you feel, would be to look back at ourselves, and see ourselves killing the thing we love.

HE DISCOVERS

he is turning into a star. His body is turning into star matter. He can see it, under his clothes. He is leaking the stuff of the universe. The Star Creature shifts in the sheets, turning to him.

Isn't this what you always wanted? she says. Aren't I everything you ever dreamed of?

She places an infinite finger into the wormhole that has appeared over his heart.

He is leaking the stuff of the universe—cosmic seepage through the hems, his socks. He picks up the star kids from the nursery. Their minder seems to know him. You're looking well, she says, singsong, this mumsy woman, hair bunned up. What's that floating up out of your collar there?

That's the stuff of the universe.

The little star girl squirms her hand in his.

He leads the star kids through a park. The star boy chases a squirrel with a stick. He finds he has snacks in his pocket, hands one to the little star girl. She takes it silently, holding it two-handed to her petal-like mouth, numming, gazing. The boy is panting, falsetto yipping. The squirrel cocks a glance.

He is turning into a star. He takes off his coat in the bathroom, his shirt. It is floating from him like nuclear smoke, reams and plumes of light, and like dust motes in a beam of sun he can see the particles. If you got up very close, she says, appearing behind him, you'd see planets in there, little moons. She looks not at all like the woman he first met, eons or possibly weeks ago. But your eyes don't really have the magnification I'm afraid. She smooths the seam of light that has opened up on his shoulder. He tries to tell her how he is feeling.

Shh, stupid man. An infinite hand brushes his face. You don't have any feelings at all.

She shaves his head for him—I like my men bald. She tells him she loves him. She tells him

You are an empty sock

and I am your foot.

You are a flaccid cock

and I am your blood.

She demonstrates her love. She does her devouring thing. And she appears to be preparing for something, some voyage. She is meditating, exercising, moisturising, mirror-talking. He overhears a language he doesn't recognize.

So they ventured into the woods, deeper and deeper. Night was drawing in, and if they didn't make it home soon they'd be stuck in the woods until morning.

Are there bears in there? asks the star boy.

Oh yes, I'd say so.

Uh-oh.

Exactly. So they'd better get home hadn't they.

I saw a bear once, the star boy says, squirming under the duvet.

Sit still please. You saw a bear?

Yeah, I saw it and... and it bit me, there.

It bit you? On the arm there?

Yeah.

Oh no, poor you. I can't see a bite though.

Oh.

He smooths the boy's hair, kisses him goodnight. The boy is a furnace, a heat generator, always hot, shirtless in winter. His smell is primal. The girl is asleep, the house quiet, suddenly as good as childless. The Star Creature does not seem to be home. He pours a glass of wine. As it enters his stomach, he feels his inner chasm. His outer crust, that had felt ready to collapse, has solidified. His eyes are lost in saturnine rings. He attends the premiere of a French-US co-production. The interesting director claims to have been working on this project for close to twenty years. It just seemed right to tell this story in English, she says. I think in space people talk in English or Russian, maybe Chinese, but not French. The horse-brown plait of her hair is draped over the collar of her blazer. She sits with poise, tall-backed, pushing fifty, handsome, in front of a conference room full of press. He tries to see her afterwards. He wants to speak with her. He is a semi-respectable critic, this is not out of the realm of the ordinary. He just wants to speak with her. He asks her retinue. Just a word—I'm a fan. He sees them asking her, her looking at him. She nods a single nod.

I just wanted to know, he asked her, once they were alone, in the post-conference crowd. I just wanted to know...

He arrives home to find she has left. There's a letter from the lawyers. The children's rooms appear never to have been occupied—small bare beds and empty shelves.

Now, she had said, silhouetted in front of his blinded window in the shit bit of Wimbledon like an illustration from an epic poem or something from a dream, this time I'm going to eat a good big chunk of your soul. She asked if he wanted to object, but he did not want to object. She advised him to count backwards through Sight & Sound's top 100 films of all time to keep him calm, but he was perfectly calm. He had been waiting to be eaten up for decades. Three decades, almost to the year. Primed and readied to want to be eaten up.

THE FORMER

Teenage Actress and the former Stuntman are moving in together. A bright little apartment on the top floor of an old stucco house off the main coffee-shop drag. There's no air con, but this has been accepted. It's cool, we'll keep the windows open. We're never home anyway.

He carries her over the threshold. His arms are even bigger now—enormous, pale, python belly things. He has to tilt slightly to make it through the door.

The teenage actress has become a twenty-something actress, and with the aid of a radical hair shift and a change of management she has been repositioned as a TV property. She is trying to be your neighbour's daughter who went off the rails but pulled it together and can now be trusted to cat-sit. It's going fairly well: in a new single-camera sitcom she plays a spunky marketing intern with borderline personality disorder. One review called her a new generation's Zooey Deschanel. The management team celebrated with lunchtime champagne, which she didn't drink because she is pretending to have quit drinking.

It's kind of weird, I mean, like... I mean like do you ever feel like it's like we were *meant* to be together?

I don't know, he says, his British accent returning, you know I don't really believe in, like, fate and all that stuff.

Sure, she says, but like *look* at it, like how we met. You were on *my* show. You showed up on set when I was the *only* one there. And then we meet again on that fucked up thriller, and *again* at that party in the Hills, and I mean like… it doesn't feel acci*den*tal, right?

I don't know, he says, squeezing a forearm tensing thing, I think it's just like you make the best out of what you find, right? She frowns, shakes her hand. His tank top is cupping his pectorals like delicious flat breasts.

She decorates—old photos of friends, vintage posters, Alannis Morrissette ('I *love* 90s'). Five rooms, into which the afternoon light filters as if through a swimming pool. She feels as if she is swimming, often, though she isn't sure what the water is made of—memories? Unfulfilled dreams? The overlaid lives of the apartment's previous inhabitants? Her anti-anxiety medication? She isn't sure. She goes to set, plays a scene in which a lascivious older co-worker pins her in a store cupboard. He'll get his comeuppance later in the season. She drives down the Glendale freeway toward the apartment in Silverlake, where the water is waiting for her. Her former stuntman is not home yet—long day rehearsing for a Hong Kong action remake. She gets stuck in traffic, the evening light playing a phantasmagoria beyond the hills, between the cars. When she gets home, she will tread water until he arrives, with his enormous reassuring body, and his gentle not-very-funny jokes. She is okay with this. The radio plays a song she remembers singing, alone, in her bedroom, at the top of her lungs, back before she was a teenage actress. She sings along again, umming the parts she has forgotten, until she is full volume, and tears are rolling. The windows are tinted—no-one will see, and there are no photographers on the freeway.

SOHO lunchtime: kaleidoscope. Faces, movers, shakers. I walk, my head my own, cool London air on its contours. Breeze in my remaining hair. Sister Ray Records, Wardour Street (no A-bomb), Berwick, Edinburgh. Five months and four jobs since Copenhägen, since

My God! What *are* you?

since

Bruises, gooseberry blue

since

thick black coffee in little ceramic cups, painted with golden flowers, and

How many times have you done that?

That? With man?

Yes. Not many, I think.

No, not so many. In my country...

since I peeled off a chunk of temple to see the street boys spit, since he told me

I sought you were beautiful.

I sought

you were beautiful

Faces in the Soho lunchtime, laughing jokers, office flirters, striding actors, back-to-back meet-n-greets. Skin over features, over muscle, bone, and deep within: the tiny stars of self. Can you see it in their eyes, in the glints? Starburst? Effervesce? Solar flare? Or can you see the prisoner, locked indissolubly within? I remember: the weight of the prosthetic, how it pushed my neck side to side, how it wanted to

drop

and take me with.

Five months and four jobs since. They tell you, in this profession, you can use your real emotions, tap into genuine pain. Or, not. You can pantomime. Anti-method. Simply wear an intricate mask, so intricate its maskness disappears. Four jobs, four different people, four different alternative-dimension versions of me. One day, we'll be able to skip between alternative dimensions. Press a button and quantum leap. It'll happen. Someone's working on it now. A whole team of someones.

The screening room foyer is happy with 2pm wine. A recognisable film critic, one from the Independent, a face from Newsnight Review. I check out the press kit: *Metronomy, an anthology of short films by a New Wave of Scandinavian directors. In Copinghagen a deformed immigrant struggles to find his place in the Danish capital, but when his hidden strengths come to the fore he is given a chance for redemption.* These things never fail to turn interesting ideas into crud.

No-one knows I'm here. One or two glances: recognition? I sit next to a quiet man. His eyes are lost in darkness. Hello, I say.

Oh, hi.

Who are you with? I ask.

Oh, um. Little White Lies, today.

That's a beautiful magazine.

It is. They must save the money they don't pay me for the cover art.

Sometimes, the only way to forget about yourself is to think about someone else. So I ask him questions, this sad film critic. I ask if he's looking forward to the film, if he knows much about Scandinavian cinema. He spirals into a spiel on Lukas Moodysson and Ingmar Bergman, on Bergmanism in modern arthouse cinema, of the unsung importance of the screenwriter, of the screen presence of Mads Mikkelsen. It's funny, I tell him, but all the men in Copenhägen look like alternative versions of Mads Mikkelsen. It's true—if you squint you can imagine you're in a city of Mikkelsen clones. He laughs into his Chardonnay. It's the first time he's smiled. He looks like a boxer recovering from brain damage.

He sits a seat away from me in the screening, his satchel on the seat between us. *Copinghagen* is the first in the anthology. That's me, I tell him, as my cursed alternative self fills the screen. I know who you are, he whispers. His breath is warm, not stale, as if he's just eaten fresh falafel. He writes notes in a leather-bound notebook, using only the light of the screen.

The cursed cliffman of Copenhägen goes to visit a woman of the night. The woman, on-screen, is a decayed beauty, quite unlike the warm and gentle actress I remember. We're in the blue-orange realm—winter window, bedside lamps. She is scared of him, at first—he wears a bag over his enormous head. But then she makes him take it off. And they have not used the first takes, the ones in which she castigates him, threatens him, chases him out. No. They have used her version. She is scared of him, anyone would be, but she overcomes this. She touches him. She speaks with him. She asks him

What's it like? How does it feel?

And I can see my cogs spinning, in the eyes, under the lines of the prosthetic, half my cogs half this alternative me, this cursed me, off-script, searching for the right reply. And it comes out, in his voice:

I... I don't know.

She looks concerned, surprised, the woman of the night, this decayed beauty, damaged beauty, rediscovering her gentle soul in the presence of this cursed man.

How can you not know? she says, and she places her hand against the granite of his exploded head matter. And he recoils, just a touch—she joins him, just a touch, and music leads us into a transition...

The room is dark in the darkness of the next scene, the sad critic's eyes aglow. I see him writing something down. Back home, my basement flat is cool and empty. I know every inch of silence and distraction that awaits me there. I realise, with a gentle revelation, that I have discovered my intention.

\ *partial resolution* \

THE NEUROTIC

sexual predator sits in the window of a New York diner
with his former love. They are talking, though we can't hear
them—she's a ghost now, seen and not heard, and his voice-
over muses on the nature of jokes and love. He is not actually
a sexual predator, the character—at least he is not intended to
be, by the probable child molester who wrote and performed
him, but it's hard to control the way that things are read.

The good guy dies off-screen, before the dramatic climax,
after an innocuous flirtation with a poolside temptress. The
screen fades to black, comes back on a peripheral cop, and
distant gunshots are heard. Our hero is no more? For real.
The peripheral cop muses on death and emptiness for the last
twenty-odd minutes, in the way the Pullitzer Prize winning
author intended.

Ben chases after the daughter of his older lover, runs to the
church, bangs on the glass—he gets her! Yes, and away they
flee, back seat of the bus, staring ahead, glee falling from their
faces and floating to their feet as they sit in sudden and silent
uncertainty. Bob has to leave Japan, without the half-his-age
newlywed, but— there she is! In the crowd, he stops the taxi,
pushes through, and as they finally clutch each other, tears

welling, he whispers something in her lovely ear. Improvised, apparently—not even the director knows what he said.

The two anti-hero cops follow the villain into a warehouse. Bad Ass Number One blasts a shadowy figure, doesn't care when it turns out to be another cop. You shot Muldrake, his partner says. That sonovuabitch is here, I saw him... and I'm gonna get him. He runs off through a distant doorway. Bang. Credits.

Acknowledgements

Aaron Kent, for believing in this work; Joe Stretch for notes and encouragement; Helen Mort and Lara Williams for inspiration and confidence-building; Mark Pajak, Anjum Malik, Rachel Genn, Kim Moore, Andrew McMillan, Natalie Burdett, Nick Royle and Pete Hobbs for feedback etc; Krishan Coupland at Neon, Phillip Elliot at Into the Void, and Sophie Essex at Fur-Lined Ghettos for publishing my work and helping me to believe in it. To Simon Clark, Dave & Vanessa King and Graham & Steph Prior for floors to crash on etc. To Yassine Guermoudi & Halima Benzdira for lockdown solidarity. To Ellis Bahl, for an air bed in LA. To Ron, Jerry and Bonnie Ringlund, and Fausto and Jessie Coello, for lovely midwestern times that helped the writing of this project. To Ali & Carlton. To my mum, for modelling love and kindness and strength for many years. To my brother.

And to Gioconda Coello, for being full of love, and for helping me to be a better writer.

LAY OUT YOUR UNREST